Also by **David Oppegaard**

The Suicide Collectors

Wormwood, Nevada

And the Hills Opened Up

THE FIREBUG OF BALROG COUNTY

David
Oppegaard

flux®

Woodbury, Minnesota

First Edition
First Printing, 2015

Cover design by Lisa Novak
Cover image © iStockphoto.com/7401919/©simonox

Flux, an imprint of Llewellyn Worldwide Ltd.

Library of Congress Cataloging-in-Publication Data
Oppegaard, David.
  The firebug of Balrog County / David Oppegaard.—First edition.
     pages cm
  Summary: "Haunted by his mother's death, eighteen-year-old Mack Druneswald roams Balrog County looking for things to burn, staying one step ahead of his grandfather, the mayor, who is investigating the recent spat of arson"—Provided by publisher.
  ISBN 978-0-7387-4543-5
  [1. Arson—Fiction.] I. Title.
  PZ7.1.O67 Fi 2015
  [Fic]—dc23
                                                    2015014186

Flux
Llewellyn Worldwide Ltd.
2143 Wooddale Drive
Woodbury, MN 55125-2989
www.fluxnow.com

Printed in the United States of America

In memory of my mother, Kayc Kline

PART ONE

The Firebug

A firebug has woken inside my heart. He feeds on smoke and char and he is always hungry, even when it appears he's asleep and his flaming eye turned inward. I have done my best to feed him well, slinging him a diet of fires both large and small, yet this has not always held him in check. In fact, nourishing my inner firebug only made him stronger, increasing his appetite tenfold and bringing all manner of calamity to myself and the semi-innocent inhabitants of Balrog County.

My name is Mack Druneswald. This is an accounting I plan to put before God, who I don't really believe in, with little hope inside my firebug heart that it'll change a single goddamn thing.

A Brief Survey
of Balrog County

Balrog County is not actually called Balrog County. A balrog is a fictional creature from J.R.R. Tolkien's *The Lord of the Rings* that happens to be shrouded in fire, somehow, and wields a fiery whip that would go nicely with my collection of gas cans, oil rags, and colorful plastic lighters.

Balrog County, however, is simply my nickname for a territorial division somewhere in the United States of America that is far, far away from any ocean. The county is dotted with seven or eight small towns, little hamlets populated by dazed white people and a sprinkling of minorities. The three biggest towns are Thorndale (pop. 38,739), Dylan (pop. 12,345), and Hickson (pop. 3,476). Thorndale has two malls, the county hospital, and a state university. Dylan has a sawmill and a bunch of seedy bars that offer free popcorn. Hickson, where I grew up, is barely large enough to maintain its own high school and is notable mostly for its location, which is a convenient fifteen minutes south of Thorndale down a four-lane highway.

Unlike the rest of our state, Balrog County is still thick with old-growth trees that the pioneers never got around to chopping down because the area's rocky soil is unfit for growing crops. The first white men to see this area were fur trappers—hard-drinking, horse-whispering, bear-fighting dudes—and most of the towns are named after trappers who either died of some horrible disease, froze to death during one of our trademark bitch-ass winters, or killed a bunch of Indians before returning to the East Coast as wealthy, wild-eyed men in pimping fur coats.

Our town was named after Alfred James Hickson, a real hard case who came over from England in 1840 looking to get rich but ended up dying of rabies. Legend has it old Alfred was out a-trapping one fine spring day when a raccoon jumped out of a rotten log and bit his leg before scrambling away, foaming at the mouth for all to see. Alfred, who was a classic frontier realist, sat down in the woods, wrote a final letter to his wife back in England, and tied himself to a tree. Thus secured, he proceeded to die a slow and lonely death, trying to drink away the rabies with gut-rot whiskey while deliriously screaming at the forest around him.

They say Alfred's rabid ghost still haunts the woods around Hickson, which shows you how intelligent "they" are around here. We have a couple of wolves, though, and so many deer that the highway between Hickson and Thorndale often looks like the floor of a half-assed slaughterhouse. Indeed. When I was growing up, my grandfather and I would go deer hunting three or four times every fall and considered it a public service. We'd head out in the dark blue of early morning with our high-tension bows, climb into a rickety wooden stand, and wait until the sun rose and it was legal to start firing away.

Back then, deer hunting seemed like a reliable pastime, a fun, arrow-filled way to spend the day, but when I was fifteen—the year Mom died—we stopped hunting altogether. I guess we'd had our fill of death for a while, even if there were more deer running around than ever, terrorizing the highways and gardens of Balrog County like the skittish sons-of-bitches they are.

The Shiny Hellscape

Last fall, roughly two months before what I shall call the Great Conflagration, I passed through the double doors of Hickson High and gave myself over once again to the shiny hellscape that is public school. I sat through the first week of my senior year, the second, and the third.

I felt numb.

Plumb stupefied.

I had no clue why I was bothering with such a charade, since I had no plans of attending college or leading anything remotely like a productive life. I'd long dropped out of any extracurricular activities, didn't have many friends, and couldn't even be bothered to work up an unrequited crush on the six or seven hot girls in my grade. Our entire school only had three hundred and ninety students—I'd seen all these fools for so long it was like hanging out with turnips that could walk and talk and enjoyed calling me Drunesdick.

Sure, I did my homework and got decent grades—A's in English, B's in most other stuff, C's in math and science—

but that was only because I didn't want to be hassled by well-meaning teachers. Class itself was the worst part—each hour was a fresh wave of white noise, a barrage of marker-board scratchings that resembled obscure hieroglyphics handed down to our teachers from some ancient race of busybody dullards. I spent the majority of class time thinking of ways I could burn the school down without getting caught (fake a boiler room explosion? Ignite something in the chemistry lab?) and laboring on the mighty speech I'd deliver when I finally lost my shit, stood up in class, and let everyone have it.

"You all suck!" I'd say, leading with a strong declarative sentence. "None of you know shit about fuck and you probably never will. You sit in these small desks, thinking small thoughts, while your brains rot inside your cotton candy skulls, slowly melting into a gooey raw hamburger-like substance barely capable of processing reality TV. You think any of this regurgitated 'education' is going to help you lead meaningful lives? Get good jobs? Fuck. You wouldn't know meaningful if it slapped you in the face with its big meaningful cock!"

Here I would pause, both to catch my breath and glare at everyone in the classroom, including the astonished teacher. The room would be filled with a particularly profound brand of awed silence, the proper response to such bold truth-telling. I'd have their attention.

"You shamble now, and you will shamble evermore," I'd continue, my voice lowered a notch, yet still razor sharp. "You will shamble throughout your small, stupid lives and when you get to the end of it all, you will find only death and more ignorance waiting for you. Memorized historical facts won't save you. Elaborate algebraic equations won't save you. Even copious amounts of oral sex won't save you. Life is a vast, horrific net, and it's caught us all. We can only trudge ever forward and hope to squeeze some small enjoyment from it before we, too, are tits-up in the dirt.

"And school," I'd conclude, "school...is...not...enjoyable."

Then I'd gather my books and materials, walk out of the classroom, and chuck everything into the nearest garbage bin. I'd imagine thunderous applause following me as I walked out of the school, a moment of supreme triumph. I pictured the school going up in flames behind me, combusting into an entire city block of fire you'd be able to see for miles and miles, a defiant signal to a blind and callous god.

Ah, daydreaming.

Good stuff!

The Pale Girl

On my eighteenth birthday, mighty September 24th, I endured another long day of school and afterward went to my part-time job at Hickson Hardware per usual. Groggy and dull-eyed, I was sweeping the store's linoleum aisles for the millionth time when the front door chimed. My boss, Big Greg, was behind the front counter reading a hot-rod magazine. Approaching him was a girl who looked around twenty and had cascading ringlets of jet-black hair and the palest skin I'd ever seen. She was dressed in a black T-shirt, black canvas skirt, black fishnet tights, and black army boots. She asked Big Greg a question I couldn't hear and he pointed to the back of the store. When she turned to look, I saw a pale heart-shaped face, dark eyes, and a nose piercing that glittered as it caught the light.

My God, she was beautiful.

I retreated to where Big Greg had pointed and circulated with my dust mop in a holding pattern. The pale girl entered my aisle. Her boots made a heavy clopping sound as she approached—*clop clop clop*—that caused my brain to spike in fluttery agitation. I straightened and squared my shoulders.

"Hello. Can I help you find something?"

The pale girl frowned and looked me over. I imagined how I looked to her—a tall, skinny dude clad in a red smock, with messy blond hair, a big nose, and large blue eyes frequently described as "intense"—and I felt the jittery excitement of a born idiot with nothing to lose.

"Something's weird about you," she said, folding her arms across her chest.

"Yeah," I said. "I get that sometimes."

"How old are you?"

I coughed into my hand, summoning all my manliness. "Eighteen. Today's my birthday."

The pale girl took a step forward, still hugging herself. She had narrow shoulders, a nice rack, and the kind of slender wrists you wanted to encircle with your thumb and forefinger and just hold for a while.

"All right, birthday boy. Can you tell me where the hacksaw blades are?"

"Mack," I said, pointing to the nametag on my smock. "My name is Mack."

"Right. Mack."

Nobody spoke for a moment and I wondered what the pale girl planned to do with a hacksaw. You could hear the florescent lights humming above our heads like tiny, demonic angels.

"Saw blades are at the end of this aisle," I announced, jerking my thumb over my shoulder. "Don't worry. We've got a fuckload of them."

The Home Front

Hickson appeared less flammable than usual as I walked home from work, wistfully preoccupied by thoughts of the pale girl, she of the metallic blades and dark curly hair. Though I was a reluctant virgin and relatively unschooled in the ways of lady folk, I figured girls like the pale girl were a little goth, a little artsy, and a whole lot of naughty. At least, that's what I hoped. How crushing would it be to grow close to such a dark angel, to infiltrate her spiky outer perimeter, and find not a freaky deeky sexpot but merely your average polite young lady with a bright future in multimedia ahead of her?

I turned onto my street. My family lived on the west end of town, which wasn't as nice as the east side but not nearly as shitty as the south side, which had both the Spruce Tree Trailer Court and, farther out, the Balrog County land-fill, where you could find yourself a hubcap or rats the size of Boston terriers. Our house was on the north side of the street and came last. A forest of maple, oak, and birch trees lined our backyard. The woods ran three miles deep and were home to all sorts of leaf-rustling critters, including red squirrels, possums, and some pretty husky beavers.

A shallow ravine served as buffer between the western edge of our yard and the woods beyond it. An elevated railroad track ran along the opposite side of the ravine, visible where it cut through a clearing maybe twenty yards wide. Freight trains rolled through the clearing three or four times a day, whistles shrieking. My sister and I had loved watching for trains when we were kids. The long-awaited passing of each train was an event to us, a happy arrival, as if we'd summoned it ourselves from the depths of the forest with our own special little-kid magic. We'd wave furiously to the engine car as the train passed by, the slipstream wind it generated buffeting our rag-doll bodies as we shouted and hopped with joy.

Our house was a standard two-story whatever with a gravel driveway running alongside its west side that terminated at a detached two-car garage. It had a large front porch, a side door that opened onto the driveway, and a narrow back porch. The house itself was over a hundred years old and tough as hell, with hardwood floors and vaulted ceilings. It had four bedrooms (three upstairs and one down) and two baths. The living room faced the street and had a wide bay window that looked out on the front porch and let in a healthy amount of light during the day.

I walked up the front steps, passed through the porch, and stepped into the musty coat hall. I could hear a TV yammering through the coat hall door. I opened the door and saw my father sitting in his leather recliner. He was watching the wall-mounted high definition TV to my right. In his late forties, Peter Druneswald was a lanky blond guy like myself. He had a sharply angular face but his blue eyes were soft and reasonable. He wore nerdy wire-rim glasses that made him look vaguely academic.

My father had his big feet kicked up on the recliner's footrest, showing off his ancient black socks. When he noticed me, he grabbed the remote sitting in his lap and turned the television down.

"Hey, Mack."

"Hey. You home already?"

"Yeah. Called it quits early today. Everybody was hung over."

Dad worked for a health insurance company in Thorndale and was friends with all the pale, pudgy dudes who worked there. The night before had been Thursday, their big poker night. They drank Heineken, snacked on pretzel thins, and called themselves the Fallen Deductibles.

"How was school today?"

"The usual blasted, gimp-ridden wasteland."

"What about work?"

"I sold a pack of saw blades to a hottie. That was something."

"Really? Good for you. My son the salesman."

"Did you know your socks have holes in them? You should get those darned."

Dad pulled the lever at his side and the footrest folded into the recliner's base with a gunshot crack. "I'll give that some thought. How about pizza for dinner?"

I raised my hands above my head and clenched my fists. "Friday night!"

Dad grinned, humoring me. "That's right, Big Mack. Nothing but the best for us."

"Cheesy garlic bread?"

"Sure. Why not?"

"Fuck yeah."

Dad shook his head sadly. "You know, Mack, if your mother was here, she'd wash your dang mouth out with soap."

"Sorry. I meant heck yeah."

Dad's eyes slid back to the TV. He thumbed the remote and reintroduced the noisy drone of the evening news to the room. He'd obviously forgotten it was my birthday, but I didn't take it personally. Birthdays had been Mom's big thing. He'd remember sooner or later and slip me some cash.

I went upstairs and entered my bedroom. As usual, I immediately stubbed my toe on a stack of books, one of many scattered around my bedroom floor like literary land mines. I'd gotten into reading real, non-electronic books back in the day and over the years I'd gone from connoisseur to straight-up hoarder. Not only was my bedroom crammed with five overloaded bookshelves and a dozen random book stacks, but I'd put several boxes of books in the spare bedroom and hidden eight more in the basement nobody else even knew about. I had my own personal ten-percent discount at the two used bookstores in Thorndale and their owners smiled happily when they saw me.

I shoved the toe-stubbing stack of books against the wall and flung myself onto my bed. After staring at the ceiling for a few restful moments, I picked up my writing notebook from my nightstand and opened it.

Story Ideas

- Man befriends chipmunk. Relationship soon sours.

- A humble plumber marries into a rich family in New England. Sleeps with every member of the family.

- The Mississippi River dries up. A man starts walking down it from Minnesota and a woman starts walking up it from Louisiana. They meet in the middle of the river and discover they both are related to Mark Twain.

- A talking baby squid appears in a toilet one day, offering free advice. The advice is terrible.

I grabbed a pen and started to ponder. It'd been a while since I'd written a new short story and none of my current ideas seemed too great. I liked writing stories but I always had a hard time coming up with an idea that didn't seem derivative. Part of the problem with reading a lot of books was finding out how lame and unoriginal you were in comparison to every other writer who'd ever lived.

Flashing upon a new idea, I wrote:

- An extraordinarily pale girl moves to a small town. She discovers everyone is an asshole zombie and must fight her way back to freedom using only her wits and her incredible paleness, which allows her to hide in the moonlight.

I tapped the notebook and looked around my bedroom.

Why not?

I rolled over onto my stomach, turned to a fresh page, and started writing. The world fell away.

———

Dad called us down to dinner an hour later. I stopped writing and listened for sounds of rustling in the room next door, where my sister was listening to truly atrocious pop music. A minute passed and the music continued unchecked. I left my room and went out into the hallway, where I stared at my sister's bedroom door. She'd taped a mini-poster of some constipated bad boy to the outside of her door and his eyes followed me like burning coals whenever I passed through the hallway.

"Yo, Haystack," I shouted. "Pizza's here."

No response. The terrible music continued to bump, rattling her door. I knocked on the bad boy's slick poster face.

"Hey."

The music lessened.

"What?"

I opened her door and the pungent scent of lavender candles washed over me. Haylee was sitting on the floor, her pencil-stick legs crossed in front of her. She had her laptop open on her lap and the glowing screen lit up her face. A bopsy brunette, she had elfin, triangular ears, a button nose, and gray eyes flecked with splinters of green. She'd gotten straight A's her entire damn life and wanted to be a corporate lawyer in New York City someday, with a penthouse apartment in Manhattan. A shark in training, this one.

"Come on, Haystack. Pizza's here."

"So what?"

"So … pizza's here?"

"I'm not hungry. I'll eat later."

I scanned the room, wondering how long it had been since I'd last visited the Haystack's lair. I saw fewer stuffed animals and unicorn posters than I remembered and more pictures of other teens I assumed were her friends. The pictures had all been printed on standard office paper and trimmed to size. Mashed together over an entire bedroom wall, the smiley good-time effect was the sort of mosaic creation you'd expect to find in the room of a serial killer.

"What?"

I looked down at again at my sister, so stern in the bright wash of her computer.

"I like your pictures. It's like Facebook for your bedroom."

Haylee looked back at her computer. I got the sense I could strip naked and start flapping my arms around and she still wouldn't deign to look at me again.

"You sure you don't want any pizza? You know Dad likes it when we eat together."

"I'm bloated, all right? Just go."

"All right, all right."

I stepped back and shut her door. The smell of lavender candle trailed me as I went downstairs and found my father sitting at the kitchen table, an untouched slice of pepperoni and pineapple on a plate in front of him. He'd gotten out the real plates and set the table with silverware and paper-towel napkins. He'd even poured us three glasses of ice water.

"Where's your sister?"

"She says she's not feeling well. Lady stuff."

Dad grunted and picked up his pizza. I sat down and grabbed a slice of my own. The pizza was from Panda Pies, the only pizza joint in Hickson. We'd had their pepperoni and pineapple so many times it was like eating homemade.

My father finished his slice and pushed back from the table. He stared at the empty chair across from him. Mom's old chair.

"Hey," I said. "Where's the cheesy garlic bread?"

"The Panda idiots forgot it."

"Oh. No prob."

I grabbed a second slice of pizza, though I wasn't really all that hungry anymore. Our house felt small and stuffy, its other brooding residents too close at hand.

It was time to venture forth.

The Radio Tower

Cell phone service isn't too great in Balrog County due to all the trees and the hills and whatever, but we seem to get radio stations all right. They're all terrible, these small-market stations, with the least terrible being the classic rock station, whose DJs at least have the decency to be alcoholic druggies who seem to genuinely yearn to get fired and head down the road again.

We had an older kid in our school named Willy Barnes who lived next to a radio tower. Willy said you could hear one of the country stations playing through their kitchen toaster at random hours of the day. When he got braces, he could hear the station all the time, faintly caterwauling in the back of his head. Taking a shower, he heard modern country. Trying to sleep, modern country. He got so sick of it he decided to get his braces removed and live with crooked teeth.

After he graduated, Willy shaved his head and moved to Nepal.

The Shack

Hickson did not take long to drive through. Darkness had fallen upon the land and the streets were empty, as if it were a time of plague and everyone had gone home to die reasonably in bed. My car, an enormous, maroon colored 1978 Oldsmobile Delta 88, rocked merrily on the road. Its dashboard was backlit in bright white, like the controls of an old-timey rocket ship, and its gas tank was accessible only by lifting up the rear license plate. Best of all, my Olds had a huge trunk where you could easily keep a spare five-gallon can of gasoline with plenty of room to spare.

I rolled my window down and leaned into the balmy night. I was going a comfortable fifty-five, in no hurry with no exact destination. I'd passed through the east side of town and headed out on CR-8, a paved two-lane that wound around fifty miles of scraggly apple farms, private houses, and a whole shitload of trees. Meth labs were rumored to operate along CR-8 but I'd never seen any myself, just a slew of tacky designer mail boxes, ugly lawn ornaments, and enormous American flags.

Twenty miles into my aimless wandering I noticed a glint of silver amid a patch of grassland to the north. I turned onto a gravel road that seemed headed in its general direction, feeling whimsically adventurous. The Olds slammed painfully on the pocketed road, its worn struts crunching even when I dropped my speed to thirty, but I took the shitty road as a good sign—it meant the road led somewhere, but not somewhere important or trodden enough to be well-tended.

The Olds bottomed out a half-mile down the gravel road and I pictured the sloshing metal gas can in the trunk, too heavy for tipping. The glint of silver I'd noticed from the highway slowly became a small oval lake reflecting the moonlight. I tapped the brakes and the Olds came to a crunching stop thirty yards from the lake's shore. I turned off the engine and the headlights and sat quietly, letting my eyes get accustomed to the near dark.

The crickets were loud. They chirped their hearts out at the crescent moon and the dotted stars and the tall grass swaying above them. The lake was smooth and reflected the moonlight like a mirror. The only structure in sight was a single wooden shack the size of a one-car garage.

No houses, no people.

Just a shack.

A cozy little shack.

I got out of the car. I could smell the skim of algae on the lake, baked all day beneath the sun. I turned in a full circle, searching the horizon for artificial light. Nothing. I opened the trunk of my car and took out the gas can.

I shook the can and listened to the gasoline slosh. The firebug frolicked in my chest, ready to light the lights.

"Hey, buddy, we don't have to do this," I said aloud, trying to reason with it. "We don't have to burn anything down."

The firebug hopped up and down, growing impatient. It couldn't speak directly to me, but it could mime like a pro.

"This is a shitty thing to do, you know?"

The firebug hopped and hopped.

"This is someone's private property," I said, gesturing grandly to the bucolic scene before us. "They probably love this old shack. Maybe their gruff yet kindhearted grandfather built it with his work-chapped hands. Or maybe when they were little kids they pretended this shack was a portal to a magical kingdom filled with dragons, elves, and chaste good times. Do you really want to be responsible for the destruction of happy memories like that?"

The firebug did not give a goddamn about happy memories. The firebug wasn't about happy memories at all. No, it hopped and hopped and grew hotter and hotter until I felt something akin to bad heartburn mixed with a handful of magma. The firebug was a natural force inside of me, like a blizzard or a thunderstorm, and you couldn't reason with shit like that. You could only hope to subdue it with minimal collateral damage.

I brought the can over to the shack and set it on the grass. I pounded on the shack's padlocked door.

"Hello? Anyone in there?"

No answer, but I wasn't taking any chances. I knocked three more times and waited in case someone was taking a nap.

"All right, shack. Say your prayers."

The shack prayed to its shack gods as I circled it, splashing gasoline along its base. The smell of gasoline was strong, real fumy. When I'd finished the dousing, I brought the can back to the car, set it in the trunk, and slammed the trunk's lid shut. I always put away the can first—I imagined most pyros got caught because they got sloppy and overexcited and ended up, sooner or later, torching their balls off. Which I found understandable, since once that old firebug started bopping around it was harder to control yourself and take the necessary precautions.

The wind died down. I returned to the shack's perimeter and took a matchbook out of my pocket. I studied the shack, a dark, boxy outline against the clear night sky, and savored the leaping in my heart. I plucked a match.

"Goodbye, old friend."

I struck the match and tossed it against the building. The match's light darkened for a second, threatening to go out, and then the gasoline caught and whooshed into flame. The firebug sang rapturously inside my chest, droning out the moonstruck crickets and sending wave after wave of electricity through my body.

The flames engulfed the shack quickly. I was forced to take a few steps back, then a few more. A hole opened in the building's side and I could see a boat inside. It looked like a small fishing vessel, with some metal framing that might have been a dock. I wondered if the gas inside the boat's trolling motor would ignite and what that would be like, if it would shoot off into the stars, like a fiery rocket, or if it would simply go boom.

The fire's intensity grew, the building's interior now white hot, and the shack's frame wavered uncertainly. The roof began to tilt and then fell in altogether, collapsing what remained of the shack's walls and crashing onto the fishing boat. I retreated farther and turned my back on the fire.

You could see the lake's shoreline as clearly as if it were daytime. My eyes stung from the smoke and the burning gas. I took off my clothes and walked into the lake, slowly feeling my way forward. The lake only came up to my knees for the first ten or twelve feet, but then I reached a drop-off and dove headfirst into the silvered water. After the heat of the fire, the lake's coolness felt wonderful and even the algae scum didn't bother me.

I swam toward the lake's center, happy in my swimming nakedness and kicking my legs in strong, convulsive arcs. I didn't look at the shore until I'd reached the middle of the lake, the exact center of the silvered water, and when I finally turned to look, the beauty of the fire, with such a starry backdrop, threatened to overwhelm me and I had to remind my legs to keep churning. The firebug and I did not want to sink.

The Good Old Days

The House of Druneswald had not always known such troubled times. We'd once been blessed with a period of goodness and light and mildly ambitious family vacations. A time when my father smiled honestly and without effort. A time when Haylee talked too much and hugged dogs on the sidewalk without asking their owner's permission. A time when I wasn't quite so dopey or lazy, and I was ignorant of the firebug's morally questionable hunger.

Sadly, I didn't fully appreciate this golden epoch at the time. The problem is that when you're little you're a slobbery, bumbling fool, happily knocking things over and ignorant of even the most basic concepts, such as the passage of time and the inevitable decay of all living matter. You simply run about and live so fully in the moment you cannot imagine the future.

When you're little, you get into all kinds of stupid shit, and the person who inevitably pulls you out of that shit is your mother. At least, that's how it went in our family, where everybody had their specialized role.

Simply put:

The firstborn son, I liked trouble and back-talking and things that went boom.

Haylee, the chirpy kid sister, was usually either my unwitting target or my accomplice. She enjoyed drama on a near operatic scale and milked it for every emotive note she could get.

Dad, the fully domesticated adult male, worked in an insurance office where the florescent blandness crept in behind his eyes all day, every day, like an invasive alien life force, and when he came home he just wanted to drink beer and watch PBS programming without being hassled.

And Mom, well, Mom was calm. A steadfast presence, Mom could step into a heated situation and sort it out with an ease that bordered on the miraculous. If you had a complaint, however morose or idiotic, she'd hear you through to the end and offer a perfectly sensible solution, whether you really wanted one or not.

You were bored?

Go mow the lawn. Only boring people are bored.

Your sister was bugging you?

Shut your door.

You hated your homework?

Fine, don't do it. You can be a bum and see how you like living in a cardboard box all winter.

My parents both grew up in Hickson, but Dad was five years older and they didn't meet until Mom was twenty-one. A recent graduate of Thorndale State with a bachelor's degree in psychology, Mom was volunteering at a church-basement dinner, scooping spaghetti out of the spaghetti vat to everybody in line when my father, a hungry young man just starting out in the insurance business, fell in love with her at first sight. Dad got her phone number, called the next day, and proceeded to court our mother with the same steady, workmanlike manner he applied to wooing a new client. My mother said she'd liked my father's kind smile, his honesty, and his outspoken dislike of war of any kind, which was a refreshing change from all the Vietnam talk she'd grown up with in Grandpa Hedley's house. They dated for seven months, got engaged, and were married within a year while already expecting me, a not-unheard-of timetable in Hickson.

Growing up, Haylee and I knew our parents loved each other and that they loved us, too. We were lucky. Our only responsibility was to be kids with other kids. We biked around the neighborhood, explored the woods behind our house, and watched trains roar through the clearing. We'd tear grass and mud from the earth and throw it at each other, laughing, and life was pretty good, pretty fucking good.

When I was seven and Haylee was old enough for preschool Mom started working on a master's degree in counseling at Thorndale State. Pursuing the degree, while raising two kids, took her an intense two years. We all went to her commencement and Mom was so happy that day she seemed to glow, outshining even the other glowing graduates on the podium. We could see she'd slain some wicked dragon in her own heart, a shadow that she'd never spoken of outright to any of us.

With her newly minted degree, Mom got a job at Planned Parenthood as a counselor, offering guidance to women, men, and couples forty hours a week. Mostly pregnancy options and post-abortion counseling, with some life coaching sprinkled in. Her calm nature must have served her well in a job like that and I can imagine her at work right now. She's holding a clipboard, small and finely boned like her own mother, and she's dressed in a sensible black skirt, white blouse, and light wool sweater. She's pretty in an understated kind of way.

When we went on car trips, Mom would point out the leaves on the trees, the birds in the air, and the signs along the road. All the shit the rest of us took for granted as bland traveling backdrop she appreciated with a childlike sense of wonder that both baffled our father and, I think, made him envious, having himself looked at the material world for so long as something that either needed to be repaired or would need to be repaired in the future.

Haylee and I took to mimicking our mother from the back seat, pointing out things and declaring in our best dopey Mom voice:

"Look at that mailbox! The red flag is up!"

"Hey, look at that dead skunk! He looks like a bloody pancake!"

"Oh guys, how about that?! Those are clouds right up there!"

"Oooh, see that? That dog is totally taking a big dump in that yard! Isn't that AMAZING?"

And so on, until Dad turned around from the driver's seat and told us both to shut the heck up already, even if Mom was smiling at our teasing, her eyes continuing to search the passing scenery for the next item of note. She had a way of caring about people deeply but not really caring what they thought about her, in terms of coolness, and this gave her a sort of Zen-type patience with asshole behavior. No matter how big the jerkwad, and no matter what manner of idiocy spewed from his jerkwad head, she could serenely stand her ground in a conversation and make her points evenly, without losing her temper. She was the one her clinic sent outside to talk with protesters, the one you wanted by your side in a parent-teacher conference.

The only problem with growing up with someone like my mother in your life is that you assume she'll always be there, listening to you and supporting you. You never expect there will come a day—say, when you're ten—that she'll come home from the doctor's office a week after her annual checkup and sit quietly through dinner, her eyes glassy and far away, and later you'll hear her talking with your father behind their closed bedroom door, which is usually never shut, or that the next day everyone will gather in the living room while your parents announce that your mother has a cancerous tumor in her lungs, a lung cancer situation even though she doesn't smoke. You don't expect your mother might someday punch out early and that her absence will turn into a vast and profound darkness at the core of your being, a nuclear winter you've stumbled into without a proper coat, boots, or even a working compass to help point you in a safe direction.

When you're little, you just think she's your mom, which to you means the same thing as eternal.

Because you're an idiot.

The Dam Store

Five miles northwest of Hickson is a town called Running River (pop. 679). Running River has a small hydroelectric dam you can walk along the top of and ponder what it'd feel like to jump into all that rushing water below. Right beside the dam is the Dam Store, which is a combination bait shop and burger joint. The restaurant section consists of five vinyl booths and five cracked vinyl stools running along a greasy soda shop counter. For some reason, the Dam Store makes the best fucking cheeseburgers and apple pie on the planet.

It's worth the drive, if you don't mind the smell of night crawlers and leeches that drifts in from the back room.

The Grotto

The morning after the shack burn, I woke feeling like a greasy, low-down villain of questionable moral fiber. I had burned down an innocent shack—a boat shack! A shack of leisure and good times!—just to subdue a make-believe creature living inside my all-too-real heart. My eyes were scratchy, my throat was raw, and I could smell smoke pouring out of every oily pore in my body. I'd become a freight train heading straight for Fuckupville.

I took a shower and ate breakfast, but I still felt like crap. It was always like this after a major burn—the build-up, the pretending-you-weren't-going-to-burn-something-when-you-knew-you-fucking-were, the glory of the burn itself, and then the horrible crash after, which made me feel like somebody had scooped out my guts and replaced them with raw sewage. I didn't *want* to be the immature dick that started shit on fire—I *had* to be him.

In need of some good cheer (and maybe a cookie), I drove over to the east side of town to check in on my grandparents. I found them in the Grotto, which is what they called their fenced-in backyard. The cluttered culmination of forty years of picky landscaping, the Grotto contained a picnic table, a vegetable garden, two flower beds, a hammock, a burbling pond, a seven-foot-tall replica of Michelangelo's *David*, and a winding stone path. The entire area had to be only five hundred square feet total and always made me think of a ship in a bottle.

Grandpa Hedley was sitting at the Grotto's picnic table. A seventy-two-year-old Vietnam vet, my grandfather had been mayor of Hickson for thirty years running. A big man with wispy white hair and a booming voice, he got worked up about stuff like grass clippings sprayed illegally into the street, fire department pancake breakfasts, and Hickson's Fourth of July parade. This morning he was holding pruning shears and studying a potted bonsai plant. Several other bonsai also sat on the table, stoically waiting for review like a tiny, carefully assembled forest army.

Grandpa Hedley squeezed the pruning shears, pondering his next move. "Hello, Mack."

I stopped short of the table, surprised he'd noticed me. "Hey, Gramps."

Grandpa Hedley gave the bonsai a snip that appeared to have no result. "The Vietcong would have a field day with a round-eye like you. They'd hear you coming from a mile away."

Grandpa Hedley chuckled and gave the bonsai another snip. This time, I thought I saw something green slightly move.

"Well," I said, sitting down. "It's a good thing I wasn't in Nam, I guess."

Grandpa Hedley nodded his head somberly. "Good thing."

I scanned the Grotto. The fountain was burbling away and filled with dead bugs.

"Where's Grandma?"

Grandpa Hedley pointed his shears toward the statue. "In back, reading one of those goddamn pornographic novels of hers."

"Pornographic?"

"You should try reading one. It's hardening member this, stiff organ that."

Grandpa Hedley gave his bonsai three consecutive snips. He set the pruning shears down and turned the tree in its little pot.

"Is that its back or its front?"

"Trees don't have sides. Trees are trees."

I nodded. Grandpa Hedley could sneak up on you like that, throwing down profound shit when you least expected it. I think it was one of the reasons he'd been Hickson's mayor for so long and had a death grip on the town's oldster vote. The way he said things made them seem like eternal truths that had been set down in stone tablets long ago, via chisel, by a man on a mountaintop.

"I got you a job at the Legion bar, Mack."

"I have a job. I work at the hardware store."

"Right. How many hours do you work a week?"

I leaned closer to the bonsai, wondering what my

grandfather was looking for exactly. I saw tiny roots, tiny trunk, tiny branches. Micro-needles that glowed with chlorophyllous radiance.

"I don't know. About fifteen, I guess."

Grandpa Hedley shook his head sadly and picked up his shears. "That's not enough work for a young man. You need more structure than that. Especially with your mother gone."

"I don't know," I said, stretching my arms. "I think I've got a good thing going around here."

"You're eighteen now, Mack. You should be working your ass off and saving for college."

I swung a leg over the picnic table's bench. "You never even went to college and you've done all right for yourself, Mr. Mayor. Mr. Backyard Grotto."

Grandpa Hedley leaned closer to his bonsai. "I didn't go to college because I was getting my ass strafed in the Mekong Delta. You don't want that kind of education, kid. Trust me."

———

Now a full-time man with two part-time jobs, I plunged into the depths of the Grotto and found Grandma Hedley rocking gently in the Grotto hammock. She was wearing her straw garden hat and olive green overalls and drinking iced tea. As foretold, she was reading a thick, greasy romance novel with raised gold lettering on the cover.

"Hello, sweetie."

"Hi, Grandma."

I leaned over and hugged her small body with one arm, careful to not squeeze too hard. Grandma Hedley smiled. Her eyes were milky blue, like stonewashed denim, and magnified crazy huge behind her trifocals. She had short cropped hair she dyed crimson and a ready smile for anybody. She looked like a kindly lady gnome.

"Did you have a good birthday? We have a card for you."

"It was pretty good, I guess."

"How's your story-writing going?"

"All right. I started a new one yesterday."

"That's lovely. I can't wait to read it. Did George tell you about the new job?"

"Yes, ma'am."

"And?"

"I start at the Legion next Friday."

Grandma Hedley lowered the romance novel to her chest and gave a speedy, hummingbird-like clap. "Oh good. I think it'll be very enjoyable for you, Mack. You'll get to hear all those stories they have. It could even help you with your writing. Maybe you'll write the next *Johnny Tremain*."

"Ah—"

"Here, help me up."

My grandmother held out her hand like she was getting out of a cab. I grinned and took it, extracting her from the fibrous web.

"You missed lunch, but I can make you a sandwich. We've got some rhubarb pie left over."

We went inside the house. Grandpa Hedley was on the phone in the kitchen. He was listening to the receiver with his good ear, his face darkening to a deep, plum-like purple. Grandma and I waited, watching him. Finally Grandpa muttered something and hung up the phone, his eyes slowly focusing as he noticed us standing there.

"What is it, George?"

"Some hoodlums burned down Teddy Giles' boat-house."

Grandma Hedley crossed her arms and frowned. "Oh dear."

The Mayor's Corner

Dear Residents of Hickson,

As you have probably heard already, the boathouse of Theodore "Teddy" Giles has been destroyed in what police believe to be an act of criminal arson.

This, of course, is a tremendous black eye for our sleepy community. Those of you who know Teddy (and who doesn't?) know about his exemplary life of service to both Hickson and the United States of America. An all-state quarterback for Hickson High back in the late eighties, Teddy led our beloved Wildcats to not one, not two, but *three* consecutive state championships.

Then, despite being offered several college football scholarships, Teddy joined the Marines and fought in the Gulf War, where he distinguished himself by taking shrapnel in his leg and still completing his mission, which was to relay a visual ground confirmation on an Iraqi troop unit in Kuwait, allowing it to be blown to smithereens by an American bomber.

His leg badly mangled, Teddy returned to our area with a Purple Heart, unable to play football or walk without a limp but still a shining example of everything fine and upstanding about being a man, a soldier, and an American.

To the coward (or cowards) who burned down Teddy's boathouse, I can only say shame on you and ask you to look deep inside your soul, which may need to be washed out with soap.

To everyone else, I ask for continued vigilance until this perpetrator is caught and dealt with appropriately. If you see anything, do not hesitate to call the police. As with any form of terrorism, *we are in this together.*

Sincerely,
Mayor George Hedley

The Firebug's
Legend Begins

Throughout my pyromaniacal history I'd sought to keep my doings well below the notice of the citizens of Balrog County. I didn't need popular acclaim, or outrage, to soothe my ego and make me feel like a big big man. My work—the controlled fires, medium and small, that I'd ignited throughout the area—was its own glorious reward, the charred ashes of various flammable objects an end in of itself.

I wasn't in it for the money, the glory, or the chattering of the townsfolk.

I was in it for the burn.

Still, celebrity often comes to those of us who seek it not. As I read my grandfather's column in the *Hickson Herald*, our town newspaper, I could not help but feel the trappings of vanity slip comfortably around my shoulders, as snug and reassuring as a king's ermine coat. Poor Teddy— how could anyone burn down his precious boathouse? How could such a terrible thing befall such a fine, outstanding gentleman?

Ha!

Because this was life, bitches!

Yes. This was life. Apparently neither my grandfather nor anyone else in Hickson had stopped to consider the idea that the arsonist involved had actually no freaking idea who owned that shack out in the middle of fuckwhere. They could not, or would not, account for the chaotic randomness of chance in the selection process. To acknowledge that Giles' boathouse was burned to cinders not because he was Teddy Giles, big-time hero, but simply because it was there, unprotected and tempting, would have been the same thing as acknowledging the fact that the universe didn't give a goddamn who you were and could turn on you in a second, which was absolutely true and terrifying and best not considered too closely, lest one go insane staring into the abyss of time and space etcetera etcetera.

And this willful blindness, I must say, got me plenty stoked up.

––––––––––

The following Wednesday, Sam Chervenik ambled into the hardware store right before closing. Sam was in my grade and basically the only dude from school I liked hanging out with or could really tolerate for more than five minutes. Like me, he was a big reader, mostly science fiction and fantasy with some Nazi Germany shit thrown in. He also didn't plan on going to college, which he considered a racket fit for mindless drones, and worked at a comic book store in Thorndale for ten cents above minimum wage. He lived with his chain-smoking grandma on the north side of Hickson, where he could stay rent-free as long he took out the garbage and mowed the lawn and did other man-around-the-house stuff. Round-faced, broad-shouldered, and intense, Sam looked like a young Orson Welles, which he took as a compliment in his own weird Sam way.

I lowered the book I was reading. Sam came up and drummed on the front counter, glancing around furtively like he was about to hold the place up.

"Hey man," he said.

"Hey."

Sam looked me in the eye. He was always looking you in the eye with mad intensity, but that only meant he was paying attention. Otherwise, he was off in his own private dream world, thinking about dragons and shit.

"How's work?"

"Exhilarating as always."

"Yeah?"

"But we close in ten minutes, so I think I'm going to make it. Another week as an employed member of the American economy."

"That's good," Sam said, nodding. "Hey, what are you doing Friday night? There's a kegger out at Lisa Sorenson's house."

I crossed my arms and leaned back on my stool. "You want to go to a party, Sam? Do you have a fever?"

Sam shrugged. "I heard there might be some girls there from Thorndale State."

"Ah. So that's your racket."

Sam wiped his nose with the back of his hand. He'd started to sway slightly on his feet, which meant he was excited.

"I don't know," I said. "I start working at the Legion on Friday. I don't know how late that'll go."

"Shit. Those old fogies go to bed around ten o'clock. You'll be out of there before eleven and I'm betting this thing's going to go until two, three a.m. There's going to be a keg and a bonfire."

"A bonfire?"

"That's the scuttlebutt, Trixie."

A pagan image of college girls dancing before a colossal fire rose in my mind, coeds sexily removing their clothes in a fit of drunken ecstasy. It was exactly the sort of event the firebug and I needed to avoid.

"All right," I said. "I'll pick you up after I get off."

"Sweet." Sam rubbed his hands and looked around the store. "Hey, you hear about that Teddy Giles thing? Is that fucking funny or what?"

"Funny?"

"I mean, my grandma never shuts up about that goodie two-dick. He makes me want to puke."

My stool creaked beneath me as I looked around my friend toward the back of the store, where I expected my football-loving, patriotic boss to emerge from his office with a howl of righteous indignation.

"You know," I told Sam, "you're all right, man."

"You're fucking right I'm all right."

Sam smirked and shot me with both index fingers, a real cool cowboy gesture. I felt a sudden urge to tell him my secret identity, to confess that I was the firebug who'd burned down the boathouse and riled up Grandpa Hedley, but Sam turned on his heel abruptly and walked out of the store before I could say anything, high-fiving the decorative scarecrow near the entrance on his way out.

The man knew how to make an exit.

After Big Greg and I closed the store I headed home on foot. As I cut through the business district's patchwork of off-street parking lots, I noticed that the grocery store's rear loading dock was stacked with cubes of crushed cardboard bound by twine. The cubes were about four-by-four cubic feet in size and twelve in number. Totally unguarded, they'd most likely been left out for pickup the next day.

I kept walking, the cogs in my brain turning as I whistled a jaunty tune.

The Tiny Door

When I got home from work, Haylee was barricaded in her bedroom and Dad was nowhere to be found. Abandoned by my family, I ate a microwave burrito in my bedroom while I checked my email. Nothing but junk and three new forwards from Grandma Hedley (a long-winded joke about a man on a tractor, a picture of a cat wearing a sombrero, and a list of twenty-five cornpone truisms), so I surfed around a bit and discovered that the *Thorndale Times* website was reporting that investigators had found a fresh shoeprint at the site of the Teddy Giles boathouse fire. It was a men's, size twelve.

I looked down at my feet, feeling a little thrill. Mmm. Not bad sleuthing. I'd be in trouble if they ever got their grubby hands on my sneaks. Next time I worked in soft terrain I'd have to put plastic bags around my shoes and cinch the bags in place with a rubber band, like a hit man in the movies.

I finished the burrito and went to the bathroom to wash up. The upstairs bathroom, which Haylee and I shared, had two sinks and a big wall mirror. The bathroom also had a toilet, a claw-foot porcelain bathtub, and a tiny wooden door set in the wall above the foot of the bathtub. This tiny, mysterious door had seemed to contain magical properties when Haylee and I were children, as if one day we might open it and discover a family of leprechauns enjoying tea and crumpets on the other side. In reality, the door led to a laundry chute that plunged all the way into the basement. The main opening to the laundry chute, an uncovered vent, was actually on the other side of the wall, set in the corner of Haylee's walk-in bedroom closet. When the tiny bathroom door was open it was possible to peer into each room from the opposite side.

Which had been fun when we were kids, since you could pop your head through the doorway and scare the shit out of anybody on the other side, whether they were soaking in the tub or hanging out in the closet. Luckily, the door had a knob on it and could only be opened from the bathroom side and as long as you made sure the door was shut you didn't have to worry about your little sister (or goblins) popping the door open and seeing you naked in the bathtub.

I brushed my teeth to get rid of the nasty microwave burrito aftertaste and washed my hands and face. As I combed my untamable blond hair I heard what sounded like a ghost murmuring in the bathroom wall. I put the comb down and placed my ear against the wall.

Our house was old. Sometimes bats got trapped in the walls—you could hear them scratching at the wood and plaster for a few days, until they either died in the wall or found a way to get out—but as far as I could remember I'd never heard a ghost before. I listened carefully, homing in on the center of the ghost murmuring, and found myself at the tiny door above the bathtub.

"Shit."

I looked at the door and its tiny brass knob. Did I really want to explore this further?

I heard Grandpa Hedley's voice in my head, telling me to man up.

"Fine," I whispered. "I'll man up."

I reached out, turned the brass knob, and slowly opened the tiny door. The ghost murmuring grew louder and I realized it wasn't murmuring at all. Haylee was crying.

And listening to Dido.

I took a deep breath and peeked through the tiny doorway. My sister was lying on the floor of her closet, wrapped in a Strawberry Shortcake blanket I hadn't seen in years. She was on her side, facing away from the laundry door and spooning her enormous stuffed panda. Nothing showy, her sobs seemed to come from a place deep within Haystack's heart, a central location where she had an inexhaustible supply of sadness she could tap at will.

Hypnotized by this display of unvarnished grief, I stood watching for a minute before I couldn't take it anymore and slowly, with infinite care, closed the tiny door again.

The Landfill

Hickson kids like to use the Balrog County landfill for parties. It's supposed to be guarded twenty-four/seven, but the night guard is a drunk who's usually out cold by one a.m. There's a hole in the landfill's fence everybody knows about and if the wind's blowing right the smell's not so bad, at least when it's cold out. The cops never sweep the landfill because everything there is destroyed already and you can find lots of cool shit if you dig around a little.

It's like a fun drinking game, sifting through all that old trash. I've heard stories about people making out and even fucking in the Fill, but I've never had the opportunity to give that a go.

Hickhenge

Harried by my sister's display of sorrow, I left the house and went out to our garage. More of a free standing aluminum shed than a traditional attached garage, it was built by my dad from a kit he'd ordered online. He'd ordered the two-car garage kit but they'd delivered a four-car kit by accident so he just built that fucker instead, setting the mammoth beast up right at the end of our gravel driveway and spreading out more gravel for the shed's floor.

Our humble shed-garage, which looked more like it belonged on a county fairground than anywhere within city limits, had seen its better days. The gravel floor was stained with oil and was home to all manner of creepy-crawly insects. The shed's rafters were usually populated by birds, which were good at shitting on parked cars, and occasionally a raccoon snuck inside and caused a ruckus.

At the rear of the shed—occupying the space of roughly two cars—was a wall of hoarder junk I liked to examine sometimes, meditating as I picked through boxes of old toys and clothes and magazines and whatever else our family didn't really need anymore but couldn't bear to part with. As I sat with the junk, which was dimly lit by the shed's single uncovered bulb, the garage door rumbled to life and slowly rolled up, letting in a batch of fresh air. I kept still as a ninja as the shed was lit up by a pair of headlights and our van pulled inside.

The headlights went out and the van's engine stopped. I could see my father sitting in the driver's seat, staring through the van's windshield. I couldn't tell if he was looking at me or staring into space. He liked to listen to talk radio and sometimes he got so into it he stopped noticing what was happening around him.

Dad got out of the van and slammed his door. "Mack?"

"Hey Pops."

"What are you doing out here?"

"Nothing."

"Nothing?"

I shrugged. Dad looked up at the rafters, checking for birds. There weren't any.

He walked around the front of the van. "You know, we should really get rid of this crap. We could rent a Dumpster and chuck it all."

"I don't know," I said. "I kind of like it out here."

Dad laughed. "You would, Mack. You would."

He reached into a box and pulled out a paperback novel. "Alice Munro. This must have been one of your mother's. She loved Alice."

We both stared at the paperback, as if it might reply in Mom's stead, but it kept its bookish silence.

"Okay," Dad said, tossing the book back into the box. "I'm going to have a beer and hit the sack. Don't stay out here too late."

"I won't."

Dad left the garage, hitting the door button as he exited through the side door. I retrieved the Alice Munro paperback and thumbed through it, hoping to come across a little note or something, some proof that my mother had read the book. I didn't find any marks but I shoved the paperback in my back pocket to add to my bedroom library anyway. I started picking through the junk again, wondering what other books I'd missed, and noticed a moving dolly wedged between an old mini-fridge and a treadmill draped in spider webs. I extricated the dolly from its dusty purgatory and gave it a few roll arounds, testing its wheels and overall sturdiness.

Yes. It would do.

I threw the dolly in my trunk and drove downtown. The parking lot behind the grocery store was empty and poorly lit by one dim and flickering sulfide lamp. I parked the Olds in the lot's inkiest shadows and rolled down my window, listening to the rustling night as the firebug made merry in my chest, excited for the glory to come. After twenty minutes I saw a police cruiser cruise by and turn onto Main Street, its engine revving as it peeled out toward the highway.

Thump thump, went the firebug.

Thump thump.

It was time for a new monument to rise, a shrine worthy of the Elder Gods and Kubla Khan. I got out of my car and went to work, hustling the moving dolly onto the grocery store's loading ramp and scooping up the nearest cube of crushed cardboard. The cube was heavy but not so heavy a true man couldn't handle it with some swearing, staggering, and painful toe-stubbing. I moved the cube down the loading ramp to the center of the parking lot and then I did the same thing with the eleven other cubes, placing them all in a ring. I worked fast and the night was silent except for my own ragged breathing.

When the major pieces were in place, I untied the twine on one cube and pulled a few cardboard chunks loose. I set the chunks lengthwise on top a few random cubes around the ring, creating a crosspiece effect that paired the cubes together.

Satisfied that I had the look going that I wanted, I returned to the Olds, set the dolly back inside the trunk, and retrieved a gas can and a rag. Humming Druid-like tones of spirituality, I went around the ring of compacted cardboard and blessed each cube with a sloshing of 87 regular-grade gasoline, making certain to leave a nice splashy trail between each piece. Then I put the gas can back in my trunk, started my car, and walked back to the ring, leaving my car door open for getaway purposes.

The firebug thumped heartily, knowing well what moment was at hand. I took the rag out of my pocket and lit it with my lighter. The rag's tip caught instantly and I held it before me, dangling it over two cardboard cubes connected by one of the cross-section pieces. "I hereby call upon all the old gods to witness this holy happening," I intoned. "I call upon them to—"

I swore and dropped the rag, which was fully lit already. It floated down and landed on the cardboard cross-section, giving me just enough time to jump back as the cubes caught fire, one after another, until the entire ring was radiant with fire.

And lo...

Hickhenge was alight.

I did a quick wild man dance, looked up at the stars to make sure they were paying attention, and sprinted for my idling car, the firebug hammering joyously away in my chest.

The Legion

The Hickson Legion was two miles north of town. Like many other American Legions across the United States, it served a multi-functional purpose: it provided a headquarters for Legion members, a dance hall Hicksonites rented for weddings and other events, and, best of all, it featured a dimly lit bar where you could get a cold beer without worrying about some damn commie trying to stab you in the back.

I'd been to the Legion before, but I'd never hung out in the bar. The bar's lights were covered by emerald glass shades, the kind you normally saw on banker's lamps, and they cast an ominous pall over the room, as if everyone who drank there had a touch of jaundice. The wooden floor was covered in an ancient, sticky film of spilt beer and the walls were lined with the mounted heads of deer, elk, moose, and one pissed-looking bear. Three enormous flags—American, Legion, and POW—hung on the wall in heavy glass frames.

When I entered the bar, five or six steely-eyed old guys turned on their stools to examine me. The bartender was a slim, fifty-ish dude with a salt-and-pepper beard, thick black glasses, and a salt-and-pepper ponytail. He would have made a good 1950s Beatnik.

"You Mack?"

"Yes, sir."

"You really eighteen?"

"Yes, sir."

He waved me over.

"Come on back. I'm Butch."

Butch turned out to be a good guy, totally mellow with a rumbly bullfrog's voice. He started me on washing beer mugs (the dishwasher was broken) and went back to chatting with the old guys sitting at the bar. The sink's warm, sudsy water felt good on my hands and I dove into the work, really washing the hell out of those mugs, and when I looked up from the sink over an hour had passed and the place had started to get busy. Not packed, but busy. More men had shown up, old and not so old, and some had brought their wives and girlfriends.

I asked Butch about the crowd and he told me karaoke started at eight.

"Really?"

"Yes, sir."

"Do I get hazard pay for this shit?"

Butch rubbed his stubbly cheek with the flat of his hand and surveyed the crowd.

"Nope. But they tip pretty good."

As far as karaoke systems went, the Legion had sprung for a nice setup. The singer stood on a small raised platform in the corner of the bar, where a karaoke stand was set up with two microphones and a TV monitor, which acted as a teleprompter for the singer. The stand was wired into a big computer-looking deck, which an orange-haired lady named Judy operated from across the room, programming the karaoke playlist from slips of paper given to her by the crowd. Three ceiling-mounted speakers cranked out the backing melodies for each song and two flat-screen monitors, also hung from the ceiling, displayed lyrics so the crowd could sing along themselves.

The later it got, the more the crowd was into it, clapping and hooting and singing along to "Piano Man" and "Sweet Caroline" and all that rip-roaring cheesy shit. I helped Butch keep the beer flowing, whistling as I darted around. I got lost in the busy flow of a bar on a Friday night, a flow I was in part responsible for maintaining, and it dawned on me that this gig wouldn't be so bad at all. The worst part of working at the hardware store was all the sitting around. You never forgot about the drag of time passing, how it pulled you under with every slow minute and stole a little bit more of your immortal soul.

You never forgot it was a job.

Lisa Sorenson's Inferno

Butch let me off early and I drove back to town. Sam was waiting for me outside his grandmother's house, sitting hunched over on the stoop. He didn't move when I pulled up, so I laid on the horn and Sam jumped to his feet like he'd been zapped.

"Jesus," Sam said as he got in, slamming the passenger door. "You probably woke the whole neighborhood."

"Do you really care about this neighborhood and its sleeping?"

"No."

"All right then." I honked the car's horn again and peeled the hell out of there.

Sam scowled and peered at the Olds' dashboard, looking very Orson Welles-ish in the electric white light, the deeper pockets of his face cast in shadow.

"Oh, I get it," I said. "You're worried about me waking your old lady. Your very, very old lady."

Sam snorted and looked out his window, smiling despite

himself. We passed the trailer court and headed south on the highway.

"So, how was the Legion? You pick up any cougars?"

"Not yet, but I remain hopeful."

"That's good. Hope is good. Hope will save us all."

I nodded, unable to tell if Sam was serious or not. It was always hard to tell with him. One minute he could be cracking wise, the next he'd start ranting about how the human race was growing water-soft and how it was inevitable that we'd all be wiped out sooner or later. Sam's parents had died in a car accident with a semi-truck when he was ten years old and he was still broken up about the whole thing, even if he never talked about it. Sometimes we drove to Thorndale to visit the sports bars and play Big Buck Hunter until the waitresses kicked us out. Watching Sam expertly kill digital bucks with a plastic orange shotgun was a magnificent thing to behold, even if he never wanted to go hunting in real life.

I turned left at a lit-up Jesus billboard. Two miles later, we came upon dozens of cars parked along both sides of the road. I slowed the Olds down and we checked out the scene, noting the well-lit house a half-mile off the road and the lurching, vaguely humanoid forms in the distance. When we reached the end of the parked cars, I added the Olds to the lineup and killed the engine.

Sam rubbed his eyes and made an "urrrrrrrrrrrr" noise. I pressed the knob that turned off the car's headlights and dropped us into countryside dark.

"Second thoughts, Sammy boy?"

Sam slumped against the passenger window. "I don't know, dude. I'm not so good at this type of shit."

I sat back. The roof's fabric was sagging so close to my face I could have licked it. "Once you get drunk enough, every party's the same," I said. "There's the loud stupid guys and the loud stupid girls and after a couple of beers everybody's best friends."

Sam straightened. "That's true."

"Trust me," I said, opening my door. "Four beers in and showing up will seem like the best decision we've ever made."

I got out of the car before Sam could say anything else. What was needed here was motion, the sort of continuous momentum that allowed bookish wallflower dudes like us to venture out into the night and enjoy the company of our fellow man, not to mention college girls. We needed to stop thinking—we already thought too much, by the minute, and it was burning our circuits out.

Sam got out, slammed his door, and staggered out of the ditch and onto the road. Cars were wedged into Lisa Sorenson's driveway like Tetris blocks. We could hear voices in the dark, girls laughing. Party people were clustered in groups of four or five all around the front of the house, smoking cigarettes and blowing smoke into the air.

Inside the house, we were bombarded immediately with hot, sweaty air and loud country music. About thirty people were crammed into the living room, shouting at each other and drinking from red plastic cups. Lisa Sorenson, a big, bubbly girl who liked everybody, stood in the middle of the room, holding court. When she saw Sam and me standing in the entryway, her whole face lit up and she came bounding over.

"Oh my God! Mack and Sam!"

Lisa gave me a sweaty hug before I could defend myself. Sam, who wasn't a big hugger, took several steps back and held up his hands in placation. Lisa laughed and wiggled her fingers at him.

"I can't believe you guys came! You never show up at anything."

I hooked a thumb toward Sam. "It was his idea. Sam cannot stop himself from partying."

Lisa smiled and nodded. "Awesome! I'm so glad you made it."

I smiled and glanced at Sam, who was glowering at everyone.

"So, like, the keg's out back," Lisa said, holding up her red plastic cup. "There's a bonfire, too. Huge one."

The firebug perked up and sniffed the air, sensing smoke.

"Sweet," I said. "We'll go check that out."

"Cool beans," Lisa said, nodding again. "Then come back and dance, you guys. We're just getting started!"

Somebody in the living room whooped, setting off a round of copycat whoops. Sam and I pushed forward into the crowd, using the noise as cover, and dodged our way through the living room, past the kitchen, and out the back door. Outside, it was quiet again. To our right, just off the back steps, sat a full-sized keg and two plastic coolers. In the distance was the promised bonfire, surrounded by a ring of people.

"Look at that keg," Sam said, pushing his way past me. "It's like a giant silver grenade begging to be fallen on."

I nodded, fixated on the fire. The roaring blaze amid the cold night. The light out of the dark.

A plastic cup appeared in my hand, filled with beer. Sam also had a beer and was smiling for the first time that night. "Here's to liquid courage," he said. "May it guide us faithfully on this cold fucking night."

"Here, here."

Sam chugged his beer. He belched and wiped his mouth.

"Damn, Mack. That's good stuff."

———

I could feel the heat of the bonfire on my face as we approached it. I closed my eyes, enjoying the dancing red light as viewed through my eyelids.

"Fuck!"

Cold beer splashed my face and ran down the front of my coat. I opened my eyes and saw a girl outlined by the fire—a short girl with dark hair. Her mouth gaped as she looked at me, trying to process my idiocy and turn it into words.

It was the Pale Girl.

"Sorry," I said, whisking the spilt beer off my coat. "I didn't see you."

"No shit," the Pale Girl said, flicking her hair back over her shoulder. "You walked right into me. Like a freaking zombie."

"And your beer."

"Right. You zombied that, too."

Sam laughed from behind me. The Pale Girl looked even prettier in the firelight than she had in the hardware store, her skin extra pale and angelic, her high leather boots more kick-ass. I could feel my fight or flight instincts kicking in, threatening to take over and fuck the situation up worse.

The Pale Girl's forehead scrunched together. "You're the hardware store guy, aren't you?"

"Yep. I'm Mack. Mackity Mack."

"Well, Mack, I'm Katrina—"

"Mack-Attack, Big Mack, Mack-a-Lack, Whack-a-Mack..."

Oh, Jesus. I was babbling.

"Sorry," I said, trying to shift gears. "You're Katrina. You bought some Vermont American plain-end scroll-saw blades, used primarily for intricate wood carving projects such as the construction of doll houses or Christmas mangers."

Katrina laughed. "Holy shit, Mack-Attack. You know your hardware."

"It's my job."

"Yeah?"

"Well, at least ten hours a week. I also work at the Legion slinging brew."

Somebody shouted at us from Lisa's house. They'd

propped open the back door and you could hear the music booming inside, leaking out into the night like a poisonous audio fog. I could feel Sam watching us, waiting to see what foolishness I'd come up with next.

Katrina looked longingly at her beer cup.

"Here," I said, holding out my cup. "Have mine."

"Your beer?"

"I only took one sip. I'm not sick."

Sam coughed and muttered something that sounded like "herpes." Katrina took the cup from me, drained it in one impressive swallow, and handed it back. "Thanks, Mack-Attack. Who's your buddy?"

Sam stepped forward.

"That's Sam. He hates people."

"You do?"

Sam nodded. "Most of them."

"I hear that," Katrina said, turning and looking back at the bonfire. "Just look at all these preppy assholes enjoying themselves. How dare they?" She pushed her hair back and sighed. "Right now a child is starving to death somewhere, I bet. Probably getting raped, too. Getting raped while starving to death."

Sam and I looked at each other.

"Okay," Katrina said, burping into her fist. "Talk to you later, Mack-Attack."

"All right," I said, looking into my empty cup. "See you, Katrina."

Katrina swept by me, leaving a faint smell of bonfire in her wake. Sam drank his beer as we watched her go.

"Well, Whack-a-Mack, at least you didn't drop your pants and wave your penis around."

"Yeah," I said. "Probably too cold for that."

We reloaded on beer, found two stumps amid the gathered crowd, and hunkered down close to the bonfire. Whoever had made the fire knew their shit—they'd started with a log cabin frame of firewood, right in the middle of the pit, and it was now the luminous core of a properly roaring fire. The heat was intense enough that everybody had taken their coats off, lending a summertime vibe to the scene, like a beach party in California.

Sam and I drank and eyed the crowd around us. I didn't recognize many people.

"Just look at all these fancy college kids," Sam said. "Slumming it with us local yokels."

A girl across the bonfire raised her hands in the air and whooped. It was turning out to be a big night for whooping.

"O Sammy Boy," I said, "the flames the flames are burning."

An ember popped and we stared into the fire. Party talk buzzed around us, loud and incomprehensible, like background noise in a movie. I thought about Sam living with his grandmother, what it must be like to go through your teens with a septuagenarian as your only trusted source of adult council.

Sam picked up a handful of twigs and tossed them into the fire. I felt an urge to whoop and dance wildly around it.

"You know, Katrina's probably one of the college girls."

"I figured," I said, sipping my beer. "She's out here slumming it with the rest of them. Patronizing our hardware stores and bonfire parties. Making the local girls jealous."

Sam shifted on his tree stump and listed to the right.

"That means she'll leave," he said. "End of this semester, maybe the end of next. Whenever she gets bored or graduates."

"Yep."

The wind picked up, whipping the fire around and sending sparks sailing into the dark sky. The countryside crickets were singing. They sounded the same as the crickets at Teddy Giles' boat shack, the same as the crickets I'd grown up with chirping below my bedroom window. The whole county was filled with these crickets, the backyards and the forests and the fields and the wetlands. We had enough crickets, mosquitoes, and deer for everybody.

Sam stood and swayed like a tree in the wind. "I'm going to get another beer. You want one?"

The back of my hands began to itch. I wanted to extract a flaming branch from the fire and run back into Lisa Sorenson's house, whooping madly as I torched her entire backwoods McMansion and sent my drooling class-mates scrambling into the night.

But that would be wrong. That would be evil, evil, evil. Ahhhhhh.

Evil.

"Sure," I said, killing my beer. "Why the hell not?"

The Siege

The doctors didn't fuck around after they found the cancerous mass in Mom's lungs. We took her to the hospital for surgery two days after the diagnosis, all of us bewildered, and we brought her home two weeks later missing half a lung and thirty percent of her stomach.

I was ten and Haylee was seven and a half. Neither of us fully grasped the enormity of the change that had befallen our family, not even after Dad finished moving their bedroom downstairs into the first floor guest room, vacating the master bedroom on the second floor. We knew Mom had gotten sick, gone to the hospital for a period that felt like a thousand years, and had returned home all sewn up. We thought she simply needed to rest and eat chicken noodle soup and eventually she'd be back to her old self again. I was old enough to know cancer was about as bad a disease as you could get, but I also knew my mother was tough as hell when she needed to be—I'd once seen her back down an aggressive pro-lifer in the produce department of the Hickson IGA, an obese slob of a man with a bright pink face. I figured she'd gone to war in that hospital operating room and come back wounded yet victorious. I pictured cancer as a dragon, a flapping, emerald-scaled dragon, and I believed my mother had sallied forth and slain it.

A month after her surgery Mom got some of her old strength back, even if she had trouble breathing and ate about as much as a sparrow. She started using the toilet on her own, then showering on her own. Dad had built a new bathroom/closet annex that attached to their new bedroom using the old, small bathroom right off the kitchen and a chunk of our back porch. It was actually a pretty sweet setup—the new room's windows had a special tint to them so the sun wouldn't fade Mom's clothes and retained heat well. Also, Mom didn't have to go down into our creepy basement anymore to do her laundry since the new annex had a washer and dryer just for her.

Mom's new handicap shower was unsettling, though. It had a big rounded ledge at the back you could sit on and two stainless-steel handrails for grabbing. It was like something you'd find in a nursing home, not a house with two kids, a father, and a mother who was only thirty-two. It had a tropical-rainstorm-type showerhead, but I never used it, not once.

It felt strange at first, sleeping upstairs with our parents downstairs. Their old bedroom felt deserted. Empty. When Haylee had nightmares in the middle of the night, she started coming to my room because she was too frightened to go down the stairs in the dark. At first I played the part of intermediary, the reluctant and grumpy guide who would turn on all the lights and walk my sister downstairs to the new master bedroom. But, as time passed, I said screw it and let Haylee sleep in my room as long as she promised to sleep on the floor. She agreed to this eagerly and would drag in every blanket and pillow from her bedroom and lay it all out on the floor like a bird's nest. Then she'd go back to her room, giggling, and return with as many stuffed animals as she could carry, dropping them into her nest and laughing as they rolled.

"Dude. All right already. Lie down and go to sleep."

"Dude!"

"Sleep."

"Dude!"

And, of course, when I'd wake up in the morning, Haylee would be lying beside me in my twin bed, her gummy kid breath all up in my grill.

The next ominous change was the arrival of Randy the Oxygen Guy. His first visit must have been pre-arranged by my parents, but to me it seemed like he just showed up one day, when I was trying to eat my Frosted O's in peace, and barged into our house through the side door like he owned the place. "Hey bud," this burly, greasy-looking stranger said to me. "I'm here to help your mom breathe."

Randy installed a large oxygen tank in the coat hall, right off the kitchen. The tank, or "compressed oxygen gas cylinder," vaguely resembled a beer keg but was slimmer and taller and weighed a ton (Randy used an industrial dolly to unload the tank off the truck's ramp and wrestle it into the house, a process that involved much grunting and swearing). The tank had a couple of gauges and spigots on it and I named it HAL after the artificial intelligence in *2001: A Space Odyssey*.

Randy attached a clear rubber oxygen tube to one of HAL's spigots and gave the other end to my mother. The tube ran fifty feet, so she could move around most of the first floor while still attached to HAL. My mother's end of the tube actually split into two tubes, like earbud headphones, and like earbuds she looped the tubes around her ears for comfort and stability before stuffing the little nostril bits into her nose. The other spigot on the tank was for refilling a portable oxygen tank, itself good for ten hours of use. My mother used a metal frame with wheels on it to roll the portable tank around when she went out of the house. That one we called R_2O_2.

My mother never truly got accustomed to her oxygen tether. It caught on stuff and if she didn't notice the catch, the line would make her head snap back, *POW*, like a dog that's reached the end of its chain. She also didn't like being seen in public with the oxygen rig trailing behind her, a rolling reminder of her frailty for all to see. She took off the oxygen halter, which I've since learned is called a cannula, whenever somebody took a picture of her.

You can click through years of photos, lots and lots of photos, and find maybe half a dozen where she's wearing that goddamn halter.

But Mom was still Mom, kind and hyper-aware of those around her. She developed a new routine, which mostly involved sitting on the couch in the living room, propped up with pillows and covered by a quilt Grandma Hedley's church group had made for her. Whenever you went through the living room she'd ask you how you were doing, what was up. In the morning, she'd inevitably hear my bedroom door open upstairs and shout, "Good morning, sweetie!" in a cheerful voice I found massively obnoxious as I shambled toward the bathroom, wanting nothing more than to piss and fall back asleep as swiftly as possible. I usually grumbled some reply to this inevitable morning greeting, or ignored it altogether.

I think Mom must not only have known how obnoxious her chirpy greeting was but found it massively hilarious, a sort of running joke between the two of us that never got old to her, especially as I plunged deeper and deeper into the roil of adolescence, an early morning automaton capable only of the most guttural utterances.

Because she was missing so much of her stomach, Mom couldn't eat a lot. She'd order a big spread, pick at it for a half hour, and finally give it up with obvious reluctance. Dad and I always joked that going out to eat with Mom was like getting a two-for-one dinner special, your meal and hers.

One of the strangest things about the siege years was Grandpa Hedley. A gruff, loud-talking dude, he'd always acted as blustery around my mother as he did around everybody else. He'd pop into your house when you were out, read your mail, and yell at you for not paying your electric bill when you returned home.

But after Mom's surgery, Grandpa Hedley was a changed fellow. While his previous visits to our house had been unannounced and sporadic, like surprise inspections, he now made it his business to show up at exactly two o'clock every Saturday afternoon and sit with his daughter in our living room. He brought Mom flowers and books and gourmet chocolates she could no longer digest. He'd sit in Dad's leather recliner and rock steadily while watching Mom from the corner of his eye. Constantly harassed by insomnia and coughing fits, Mom would usually be bone-tired and on some kind of pain medication, which only enhanced the loopy aspect of their conversations.

"LeRoy Higgins hit a fire hydrant last night with his truck."

"He did?"

"He was drunk as a skunk, too. One of the deputies had to haul him in."

"Really?"

"I always told LeRoy he should watch it with the boozing. Dumb son-of-a-bitch is going to pay for it now."

"I always liked fire hydrants. I like red."

"I mean, hell. How do they expect me to keep this town running smoothly if fools are driving around soused and slamming into valuable city property? Yes, sir, I wouldn't mind taking the strap to Higgins for a good ten minutes. Or caning. Public caning's not such a bad idea."

"Candy canes are red. Red and white."

"That's right, sweetheart. They sure are."

Grandpa Hedley's visits normally wound down after a half hour or so. After a steady stream of chatter he'd abruptly fall silent, as if somebody had thrown his talking switch, and pop out of the recliner. He'd throw his strong arms around his bony daughter, kiss her cheek, and stride swiftly out of our house without a word to anyone else, his eyes wet and distant. In his absence, the house would feel as if a tornado had just swept through it and Mom would sleep for a solid two hours on her couch, which was amazing for her. Even Dad had to admit the old guy could be a sweetheart, if you got him in the right company.

———

Bacterial infections began to creep into Mom's lungs more and more frequently. The surgery had reduced her immunity and even a common cold was dangerous. The doctors gave her a variety of antibiotics of ever-increasing strength, turning back the hordes of bacterial invaders one by one. Haylee and I did our best to ignore these bouts of infection, had in fact learned to tune out every possible conversation regarding Mom's medical condition as a form of emotional self-defense, but we were still constantly aware that the siege was not only continuing, but slowly growing worse with each passing day. The idea that Mom would die young still seemed impossible, yet the idea that she'd continue to live in her current condition seemed almost equally impossible.

One night, when I was thirteen, my father woke me up in the middle of the night. He was taking Mom into Thorndale for help with her breathing, he said, his voice surprisingly calm. He wasn't going to wake Haylee, but he wanted me to know in case I woke up in the morning and they weren't home yet. He wanted me to know what was happening and to look after my sister.

"Okay," I said. He said good night and exited the room, leaving me alone in my bed to stare at the ceiling. I heard his voice downstairs, saying something to Mom, and then I heard a door slam shut. I felt small and helpless and wondered what the world would be like without my mother.

She could die, she could die. She could die that very night.

I fell back asleep.

Chompy

The morning after the party at Lisa Sorenson's I woke with my head aching and a slobbering hound licking my face. His enormous tongue was coarse, his breath foul and meaty. I struggled to get away, but my arms were knotted beneath the blankets and apparently someone had shoved an ice sword into my brain, making it hard to think even at a deeply instinctual level. I recalled the party at Lisa Sorenson's the night before, the chugging of many a crappy lite beer. A slow, creeping drive back into town with Sam as I sat hunched behind the wheel of the Olds, terrified of cops.

Too much light.

Too much slobbering.

I made a croaking sound and thrashed around beneath the covers, finally prying one arm free. I shoved the beast's hairy snout away as laughter came from the foot of my bed, wicked and merry. It was Dad.

"What do you think, Mack? I think we should call him Chompy. Because, you know, he chomps."

Right on cue, the dog chomped on my free arm. Not too hard, not too painful. Just strong enough to let me know he was good at it. I cracked open my bleary eyes, letting more horrible light flood in. The cur was a devilish blend of lab and Border collie, mostly black but with a white ruff and white front paws. A gentleman's hound complete with formal attire.

I shook my arm. The beast seemed to actually be smiling at me while the better part of my forearm was crammed into his maw.

"I see where this is going," I said. "You're one of those motherfuckers."

The beast growled, low in the throat but soft and buttery, like he was only playing, hardy-har-har. He let go of my arm and panted happily, sending a fresh gust of meaty breath my way. I wiped the drool from my arm and tucked it back under the covers, where it would be safe from further mauling. Dad gave Chompy a scritch behind the ears and both of them grinned, having a real moment together.

"I picked him up from the animal shelter this morning. Thought I'd give him to Haylee."

"Haylee?"

"She's always wanted a dog and I thought finally having one would cheer her up. She could take him for walks and stuff like that. It'll get her out of that damn bedroom."

A wave of sloshing hangover nausea swept through my guts. I tried to remember the last time Haylee had talked about getting a dog. When she was ten, maybe?

"Sure, Dad. Yeah."

Dad beamed and gave Chompy a fresh scruffing. "I thought we could spring Chompy on her together. I'm going to make family breakfast."

"Family breakfast?"

"Yes, sir. Any requests?"

I closed my eyes, wishing I could disappear into a different realm. Perhaps somewhere deep, deep underground, like the Mines of Moria.

"Coffee. Coffee would be good."

"You got it, kid. You're looking rough there. They work you too late at the Legion? You don't have to take that job, you know. You can feel free to tell Grandpa Hedley to shove it where the sun don't shine."

"Right. And then he'll beat me to death with his bare hands. Good plan, Dad."

My dad chuckled and whacked Chompy on the butt. The dog leapt off my bed and bounded out of the room.

"The old man been telling you war stories again? Heck. If only half of what he says is true, he's the real live Rambo. You take everything he says with a pound of salt and spit it out again if it don't taste right."

"Wouldn't a pound of salt make anything taste weird?"

Dad stared at me. "All right, Mr. Smart Mouth. See you downstairs in five."

———————

I stumbled downstairs and valiantly made it to my chair in the kitchen. Dad set a mug of coffee in front of me and I drank greedily from it, cupping the warm mug between my hands. Chompy, who was lying in wait beneath the kitchen table, gummed happily on my bare foot, his tail thumping against the floor. Dad was at the stove and working three frying pans, rotating between hash browns and bacon and cinnamon pancakes, short-order style.

He was actually whistling, too. Whistling while he cooked.

"Good old family breakfast, huh Mack?"

I nodded and drank more coffee. I wanted to be buried in hot coffee, swamped with it until it came out of my pores.

"Remember when we used to have these every Saturday morning? Your mother liked her bacon charred. Stank up the whole kitchen with smoke. I had to open all the windows, and still..."

The pounding in my head was slowly receding as the coffee took effect, neutralizing a few of the evil boozing cells. Chompy stopped gnawing on my foot and scrambled to his feet beneath the table. Haylee had appeared in the kitchen doorway, dressed in an old purple bathrobe.

"Hey, sunshine," Dad said. "Good morning."

Chompy exploded from beneath the table and scrambled toward my sister, his toenails clacking on the linoleum floor. Haylee screamed and brought her hands up, pushing the dog away as he lunged toward her groin.

"Chompy, down!" Dad shouted, shaking his spatula at the dog. "Down, boy, down!" Chompy gave a few more friendly lunges, Haylee kept pushing him down, and finally he gave up and did some happy circles around her instead, nuzzling the backs of Haylee's knees with his snout. She tried to swat him away but Chompy, who'd obviously dealt with critics before, dodged her hands with ease and did his best to rub his entire side against her, like a cat.

"What the hell?" Haylee said, scowling as she tried to create distance between herself and the beast. "Why is there a dog in our kitchen?"

"Dad got him for you."

"What?"

"I thought you could use some cheering up," Dad said, theatrically flipping a pancake and catching it with the pan. "You've seemed down the last couple weeks."

Haylee's jaw tightened. "So you got me a dog?"

"And food," I said, pointing my coffee mug toward Dad and the stove. "Family breakfast, dude."

Chompy, his attentions scorned, sat on the floor and stared up at my sister longingly. Did the mutt know, somehow, he was supposed to be hers from now on? It seemed like it, but that was giving the furry idiot a lot of credit. Maybe he was just drawn to people who hated him. Maybe Chompy took all that hate, internalized it, and turned it into drool.

Haylee groaned. She was hesitating in the doorway like a sparrow ready to take flight.

"But we don't do family breakfast anymore. We haven't in, like, forever."

"Well, we're doing it today," Dad said, turning back to the stove and pushing around the hash browns. "Get yourself a glass of juice and pull up a chair, little lady. The bacon's almost ready."

Haylee looked from Dad to me to the dog and back to Dad again. You could feel the charge inside her building, filling her body like a ball of heat lightning.

"Mom's not here. We can't have family breakfast without Mom."

"She's here in spirit, sweetheart—"

"Fuck spirit. I'm not eating family breakfast and I don't want some stupid fleabag dog."

Haylee turned and rushed out of the room, the hem of her robe catching air and fluttering behind her. We listened as she stomped up the stairs and slammed her bedroom door.

Dad turned off the stove burners. "What the heck is wrong with that girl?"

I shrugged and brought my plate over to the stove. "Fill'er up, sir. I'm here to report for family breakfast."

Dad laughed. He filled my plate and then his own, wielding a spatula with surprising grace. We sat down and the dog settled back under the table, where he prodded us with his snout and breathed noisily, praying for scraps. Dad and I dug into the food, elbows on table, and we ate that breakfast like it was our job.

After I loaded the dishes and started the dishwasher, I brought Chompy upstairs and led him to my sister's bedroom door.

"Be good," I told him. "Be good you crazy, slobbering beast."

I turned the knob on Haylee's door and cracked it open. Chompy hustled immediately into the breach, his black tail wagging, and disappeared into the shade-drawn darkness beyond. I wished him luck.

The Tornado

Balrog County gets its fair share of tornadoes. The worst twister in my lifetime showed up when I was twelve and home alone while the rest of my family was shopping in Thorndale. I was watching a movie when my mother called and told me to get in the basement immediately—a tornado had been spotted south of town. Right as she called, the town's emergency sirens sounded and my skin started crawling like it wanted to head off on its own.

I told my mother I'd go into the basement ASAP but instead I went outside and stood in the driveway. The sky had turned a surreal lemon-yellow and an enormous cloudbank was approaching from the south, dark as night and as big as a Magisterium Zeppelin.

The wind was blowing like crazy.

I felt alive, every nerve.

Firewall

The Saturday night crowd at the Legion turned out to be a collection of sullen old men with rough hands and furrowed brows. They sat around the bar in ones and twos, staring into the bar's majestic collection of Budweiser-themed mirrors. They spoke in low, guarded tones, like political radicals, and broke abruptly into lung-rattling coughs.

"Regulars," Butch said, nodding to the room. "They wouldn't sing 'Sweet Caroline' if you held a shotgun to their head."

One old coot named Ox Haggerton sat in the middle of the bar by himself, directly in front of the taps. Haggerton kept himself propped up very stiffly and seemed to constantly be in the process of lowering his drink (whiskey neat) or raising it to his lips. His face was so wrinkled it was puckered, like an anus, and his nose was beet red from half a century of drinking. I never saw him turn to his right or to his left but I could tell he was listening to every conversation in the bar, his hairy ears perked like a cat's. Whenever

I crossed his line of sight I could feel Old Man Haggerton's eyes burning a hole through my forehead, searching for what, I did not know.

Finally, around midnight, Haggerton stood up and pushed his bar stool back. The old man hadn't tipped me all night, paying for each whiskey as it came with a series of damp one dollar bills. He cleared his throat, a sound somewhere between phlegm and standard German, and glanced around at the other regulars.

"He's George Hedley's grandkid, right?"

The regulars nodded and murmured amongst themselves.

"Well, kid don't look like no veteran to me. He looks like a goddamn pansy boy who thinks he's smarter than a whore."

The regulars chuckled. Butch came down from his spot at the end of the bar, holding his hands up. Haggerton waved off the bartender and started for the door, surprisingly steady on his feet.

"Go fuck yourself, hippie, and cut that faggot ponytail while you're at it."

The regulars fell silent. Haggerton crossed the room, paused to sneer at us, and shouldered open the door, meeting my eyes as he plowed his way out into the night.

"Fucking dickhead," Butch said after the door had swung shut. "He gets mean drunk every Saturday and thinks it's his goddamn American right because he served two years in Korea flying a helicopter."

I grabbed a rag from under the sink and wiped down

the bar. I thought about helicopters and high grade explosives and how Ox Haggerton lived eight miles north of the Legion, on land he'd cleared himself by chopping down every tree he could get his hands on. Everybody in the area knew where Ox lived because he'd planted a sign on the main highway, advertising firewood for sale, but as far as I knew nobody had ever needed wood bad enough to visit his house and put up with his grumpy-ass bullshit.

Haggerton must have been lonely, living out there by himself like that.

Maybe he could use a visit.

After Butch and I closed the bar and divvied up the night's meager tips, I hopped into the Olds and headed north, shouting along with the radio. I pulled out my lighter and thumbed it a few times, enjoying the small lick of flame and how it reflected off the windshield's dark glass. I wasn't sure I was actually going to do anything at Haggerton's place, really, but I told myself it wouldn't hurt to take a little survey of the property. A little recognizance gander.

Of course, I was a master of hiding my real pyro intentions, even to myself. I was good at pretending I was just being weird, just fucking around, before the firebug suddenly reared up and smacked the good sense out of me. The urge to burn shit always bubbled below the surface of my thoughts, like magma flowing beneath the earth's crust, but it took a good opportunity and a sudden loss of willpower to really set me off.

Ox Haggerton's sign appeared abruptly amid the pine trees that lined the highway, a square of ghostly white with black block lettering. The old man must have gotten the sign professionally made back in the day. It'd been on the side of the highway for as long as I could remember.

GOOD FIREWOOD FOR SALE—CHEAP!
SECOND HOUSE ON THE RIGHT

I turned left at the sign, leaving the paved highway for a lumpy gravel road. The Olds rocked, creaking like a horse buggy, and I slowed to twenty miles per hour to keep the rust bucket from tearing itself apart. I also turned down the radio because it now seemed too loud, out here in the tree-ridden boonies where it was dark as hell.

It took five long, bouncing minutes to reach the first driveway and ten more to reach the second. The pine and birch trees, which up until now had run thickly alongside the road, disappeared on my right. They were replaced by sawed-off tree trunks that protruded from the ground like blunted teeth, the handiwork of a man who clearly didn't care for trees, could handle a chainsaw, and had plenty of free time.

I kept driving, slowly, and went past Haggerton's mailbox and the single lamp that lit the driveway's entrance. With the trees leveled, you could see Haggerton's house about fifty yards down the gravel road, a couple of windows still lit up, and beyond that a rectangular building that looked like a shed. I drove until the trees reappeared on the right side of the road and swung the Olds back around. I turned off the car's headlights and lowered her speed even further. "Easy does it, baby," I whispered, patting the Old's dashboard. "This is a black-ops mission."

I brought the car just short of the clearing and parked it in the middle of the road. I got out and went around to the trunk, surprised at the quiet—even the crickets were subdued tonight, as if they knew some heavy shit was about to go down. I popped the trunk and stared at the gas can. It looked so red and shiny, like fire itself.

I picked the gas can up.

Mmm, gasoline. The closest thing to liquid fire. Wars had been fought over it. Cars combusted it. It made the unholy world go round. I unscrewed the gas can and took a long, woozy sniff. I pictured Ox Haggerton sitting at the bar, drinking his beer and being all surly and shit. Calling me a pansy boy. Telling Butch he looked like a faggot.

Didn't he know a faggot was actually a bundle of sticks used as kindling in the burning of heretics?

I took another whiff of gasoline and screwed the cap back on. I pictured Ox Haggerton sitting on his pile of firewood like the dragon Smaug, hoarding his precious gold beneath the Lonely Mountain.

Fucking Smaug Haggerton.

I started toward Old Man Haggerton's house without closing the trunk, the gas can sloshing in my hand. I decided to cross the maze of tree stumps and avoid the lit driveway. It was like walking through a field of land mines that had already been detonated, annoying in a sloggy, tripping way. I had to walk with my head down, watching my feet. It wasn't until I'd cleared the field and could properly raise my head that I realized that the boxy structure behind Haggerton's house wasn't a shed. It was the largest woodpile I'd ever seen.

"Holy fuck."

I craned my head back, trying to take it all in. All the sweet, sweet stacked wood, piled high in neat little rows.

And it would be bone dry, too. It hadn't rained in Balrog County for weeks. The drought was all the local boys could talk about when they came into the hardware store.

"Steady, Mack," I whispered to myself. "Steady, old boy." I took a couple of deep breaths and waited for the firebug to calm down. I looked at Haggerton's house and realized the interior lights had gone out, leaving only the exterior porch light on. The gas can sloshed promisingly as I started forward again, circling around the back of the house like a good ninja, sticking to the dark and feeling my way forward. I cleared the house, crossed another fifty yards of tree stumps, and found myself at the foot of a pyromaniac's wet dream.

I reached out and touched a cord of wood, one among many covered in rough, dry bark. It felt as if I were stroking a mummy's cheek.

"Hello there. I'm Mack. I've come to—"

A round shape leapt out of the woodpile and dropped to the ground. I swore and jumped back, falling on my ass and dropping the gas can. A huge, very pissed raccoon chittered at me, scorning me for my intrusion. Even in the dim light I could see it puffing itself out like a devil's pompom, ready for battle. I scrambled to my feet and held out my hands.

"Sorry—"

More angry chittering. For a terrifying moment, I expected the raccoon to jump at my face and claw my eyes out.

"It's cool, man. We're cool."

I reached into my pocket and pulled out my lighter. The raccoon watched as I thumbed the lighter and held the flame toward it.

"See? That's fire."

Jesus, it was big. The size of a bull dog, really. What the hell was it eating around here? Elk?

I took a tentative step forward. The raccoon chittered again, but with less certainty now, and when I took another step it backed away, watching me as it slinked along the woodpile.

"Go on, man. This shit's about to get torched."

The raccoon turned tail and ran off into the night. I exhaled loudly and looked at the house, praying the windows would still be dark.

They were.

I picked up the gas can and went around the woodpile, using the pile's bulk to shield myself from Old Man Haggerton's house. I could see a dude like Haggerton being paranoid, restless, and prone to the kind of night terrors that made a man leap out of bed and scream into the profound darkness of his country house.

The woodpile must have been forty feet long and twelve feet high. Haggerton had strapped tarps across the top of the pile, protecting it from direct weather. The wood smelled old and moldy, but not so moldy it wouldn't burn. As I walked its length, I imagined the pile's heyday, back when the cords of wood were freshly cut and stacked, sap dripping from their wounds. It must have been twice or even three times as big back then. It probably blocked out the damn sun.

I splashed gasoline on the woodpile's far eastern corner. I wouldn't have enough fuel to douse the whole thing properly, so I'd have to settle for little patches placed at intervals around the woodpile's backside.

The can gurgled happily as I worked. Once I'd nearly emptied it, I yanked a splintered cord out of the pile and doused its knobby end. Then I looked around, considered the safety of the burn, and saw that beyond the woodpile lay only more ugly stumps stretching far into the night in all directions, like the littered battlefield of some brutal woodland war. This setup was too perfect not to burn. The old man was asking for it. Maybe he dreamt of a great fire himself, between the stretches of night terrors. I lit my makeshift torch and craned my neck back to take in the woodpile in all its sweet immensity.

"You shall be seen from the heavens, my friend."

The world felt hushed and calm and right. The critters

were hunkered in their dirt burrows, the birds nestled in their twiggy nests.

I touched off the first gasoline patch and it whoomped immediately, the fire taking nicely to the old wood. That sound, that sound. I stood still for a moment, mesmerized by the blossoming fire, until a loud crackling brought me back to the moment. I touched off the other patches of gasoline, bopping each of them like a fairy godmother with her magic fire wand, and then stuck my torch back into the pile, wedging it between two blocks of wood so it could go up with its brothers.

I could already feel the heat rising. I grabbed the gas can and backed away, careful to watch my feet among the stumps. I walked around the pile until I could see Old Man Haggerton's house. From this side you couldn't see anything burning yet, only an orange aura along the woodpile's top.

I headed back, keeping to the dark as I navigated the stumps. By the time I reached the road, the fire had spread to the front of the woodpile and was catching in earnest. The firebug cavorted about in my heart as flames ate at the last patches of dark within the woodpile and the burn entered its second, all-consuming phase, illuminating Old Man Haggerton's yard like the torch of Paul Bunyan himself.

I laughed and raised my arms in the air. I imagined I could feel the fire's warmth and thought what a shame it'd be that I'd miss watching it burn all through the night and into the morning, until nothing but forty feet of hot coals remained.

Yes, sir. Who was the smart whore now?

The front door of Haggerton's house flew open and the old man stepped outside, holding a deer rifle and wearing actual honest-to-god long johns. He strode off his porch slowly, approaching the burning woodpile like a man walking in a dream. I wondered if he was thinking about the loss of his property, various courses of action, or if he, like me, was flat-out stupefied by the sight of an actual wall of fire rising amid the dark of night.

Was he amazed?

In awe?

Did he, hardened lifelong bachelor asshole, still think in terms of beauty at all? Or was everything only function at this point?

I walked to my car and tossed the gas can into the Oldsmobile's trunk. I shut the trunk softly, got into the car, and started the engine, fluttering the gas pedal slightly so the old girl wouldn't stall on me. I rolled down my window and accelerated slowly, leaving my headlights off (I didn't need them to see, anyway, since the fire had turned the road's gravel a toasty shade of orange) as the Olds purred down the road.

I couldn't see Haggerton now, even with all the lovely firelight, but I did hear a loud crack followed by something pinging off the trunk of my car. I decided to pick up the pace, potholes be damned.

Letter to the Editor

Dear Editor,

I am the firebug recently mentioned in this very paper. Yes, it is true. The firebug speaks!

I am writing to you (and to your readers) because this is America and I believe everyone should be allowed to express themselves freely, even if it is only within the pages of a banal small town rag. Many aspersions have been laid upon my metaphoric doorstep recently, some warranted, some not, and I am well aware that the court of public opinion is not well-disposed toward me at the present time.

And, while I feel no special need to defend myself or explain my actions, I do feel compelled to respond to Mayor Hedley's recent "The Mayor's Corner" piece. In said piece he shamed me (for I am the firebug) and urged me "to look deep inside (my) soul, which may need to be washed out with soap."

My reply, in turn, would be to ask our beloved mayor if he truly believes it's possible to know the soul of any man. Because I have my doubts, people. A man's entire being is an impenetrable mask (and don't even get me started on women), with as many layers as an enormous onion. You can peel away one, two, even twenty layers, but always another layer is waiting below the surface, hungry for its turn in the sun. Some of those layers are wicked, some noble, but most of them just want to watch TV and drink beer.

So don't pretend to know me, Mr. Mayor. You do not. You would not know me if I walked up to you and threw a banana cream pie in your wrinkly face. I am a ghost and I will haunt this town for as long as it suits me. I am neither young nor old—I am the wind that stokes the great cosmic fire and fans the flames of freedom.

I am eternal.

I am the firebug!

The Firebug's
Legend Grows

We were eating dinner on Tuesday evening when Grandpa and Grandma Hedley pulled into our driveway. Their white Chevy pickup had an extended cab and was comically massive, about as necessary for the two old retirees as his-and-hers matching rocket launchers. Dad hated the truck, saying it was a showy thing to drive, but I'd always appreciated old people flair and encouraged it whenever I could.

The Chevy stopped in front of our garage. Haylee turned to look out the window.

"Hey. It's the g-rents."

Dad pushed his chair back, already frowning. He went into the central hallway and Chompy bolted after him, barking his head off. I continued shoveling spaghetti into my mouth, trying to finish dinner before whatever was going to happen happened. The side door slammed as Dad and the beast went outside.

Haylee turned back to the table. "What do you think they want?"

I shrugged and kept chewing. I had a bad feeling about where the night was headed. My firebug senses were tingling.

"I mean, they never come over here, right? Not since the funeral."

I nodded. Grandma Hedley had come over a few times to help sort through with Mom's possessions, but as far as I knew Grandpa Hedley hadn't been to our house since her death. I pushed back from the table and went to the window. Dad and Grandpa Hedley were conversing while Grandma Hedley fussed with Chompy. Grandma was smiling, so I decided their visit couldn't be that serious.

Dad noticed us watching and waved us outside.

"I hope he's not going to make us help rake their yard again," Haylee said. "I had blisters for a frickin' week."

We went out to the driveway. Grandma Hedley hugged us both, smelling like lavender water and juniper bushes. It was warm for early October and nobody had a coat on.

"We're going to a town meeting," Grandpa said. "We'd like both of you to come with and see what it's like."

"If you're not busy," Grandma said.

Haylee and I looked at each other. This was a new one. "Town meeting?"

"A special assembly," Grandpa said. "About the deviants."

"The arson, George means."

"They know what I mean, May. The whole town has been blabbing about it."

Everybody fell quiet. I sensed Haylee trying to come up with a way out. Chompy chased his tail and we all watched him go for it.

"Sounds fun," I said. "Let's check this assemblage out, sis."

Haylee scowled and gave me a look. A minute later we were rolling with our grandparents in the monster Chevy, looking down on the leafy streets of Hickson while Grandpa complained about the lawns that needed raking and Grandma told him it was all right, it was a free country.

The town hall was a big room attached to the town library. The hall had a vaulted ceiling, a bunch of chairs lined up in neat rows, and a podium placed between two oak tables where the city council sat. As we entered the room, Grandpa Hedley peeled away from us to join the council members up front while Grandma Hedley led Haylee and me across the room, making sure everybody saw her two grandchildren by her side. We sat at the end of the front row and I made sure to get the aisle seat in case somebody broke out the pitchforks and I needed to book it. About thirty people had shown up and some actually appeared to be under the age of sixty. Who were these people? How bored did you need to get to attend a Hickson town meeting?

The city council members took their seats. Grandpa Hedley stepped behind the podium.

"Good evening, everyone. Thank you for coming."

The room rustled and somebody coughed. Haylee fiddled with her cell phone beside me, texting some numb-nuts.

"I called this meeting because I wanted to brief everyone about the arsonists that've been terrorizing our county."

The firebug went pitty-pat inside my chest.

Terrorizing?

Really?

"There have been three known incidents to date. First, as many of you already know, Teddy Giles' boathouse house burned down two weeks ago."

The crowd murmured. Poor Teddy.

"Second, last Wednesday night there was an elaborately staged fire behind the grocery store in what appeared to be a Satanic-type ritual."

More murmuring from the crowd while I snorted and bowed my head.

"Thirdly, late this past Saturday evening, someone torched the big woodpile behind Ox Haggerton's place."

No murmuring this time—Old Man Haggerton could go fuck himself.

"In all three incidents, the investigator determined the fires were started with automotive gasoline using the same sloppy, amateurish method at each scene."

I leaned forward. Sloppy? Amateurish? What the hell was he talking about? Each one of those fires had been set up with love and precision! Sure, perhaps I'd used more burn juice than was strictly necessary—

Ahhhh. The sly old soldier was trying to poke the hornet's nest. He thought the firebug might be right here, at the meeting, and he reckoned that anybody who'd stage something like Hickhenge would likely be a perfectionist.

Very tricky, old man.

Very tricky.

Grandpa Hedley set his hands on the podium and leaned toward the audience.

"You know, I knew some firebugs in Vietnam. They were real gung-ho fellas, always ready to jump out from the sandbags and let'er rip. They loved big fires and big explosions and seeing the sky light up in the middle of the night. They lived for that kind of thing, I suppose you could say."

The Mayor covered his mouth with his fist and cleared his throat.

"As far as I recall, most of those firebugs ended up coming home in a body bag. That is, if there was a body left to ship home at all. Sooner or later, no matter how fast they were, or how much firepower they carried, they ended up making one little mistake and getting blown to hell."

The Mayor paused. Nobody rustled. Haylee had stopped texting and was watching our grandfather like she'd never seen him before.

Maybe she hadn't.

"All right then. I just wanted you all to know that we're taking the arsonist seriously. We've approved temporary overtime for additional police patrols and are asking for volunteers for a neighborhood watch. Hickson has never need a neighborhood watch before, but I suppose times are changing. If you're interested in joining the watch, please let Patty Saunders know. She's got a sign-up sheet with her tonight and would love to get as many names down as she can. You can choose to volunteer twenty hours a week or one hour, it's up to you. Otherwise, please let me or Sheriff Tillman's office know if you see anything suspicious. Thank you and have a good night."

The Mayor picked up his notepad and stepped away from the podium. Somebody started clapping in the back of the hall and soon everyone joined in, even Haylee, even me. I clapped and clapped and clapped, a goofy grin spreading across my face. If my grandfather wanted one more battle, who was I to deny the old soldier?

I noticed Haylee had turned to give me another look. The crowd had dispersed, but I was still clapping.

A Country Drive

The drought continued into the second week of October. The skies remained clear and blue and the county turned various shades of rust. Burn permits were denied, fallen leaves piled up in desiccated mounds, and honking Canadian geese passed through town on their way south for the winter. The temperature fluctuated daily, warming to as high as eighty degrees and dipping to thirty-five. The lack of rain appeared to have thrown Mother Nature for a loop. She knew winter was on the horizon, one way or another, but she could only stagger toward it while the birds and squirrels hunkered down, trying their damndest to remember their training.

On a warm Monday I decided to take a new path home from the hardware store, circling back through the east side of town. Though it'd always been cool to rag on the "nice" part of Hickson, all us west-side kids had secretly envied the east-side kids and their well-kept two-story Victorians, with their tastefully used Volvos and BMWs parked in the drive and their handsome fathers out puttering in the yard on weekends, wearing faded college T-shirts or cardigan sweaters, their attractive mothers carrying out trays of lemonade and brownies to anybody who happened to be around—even you, a west-side kid so bored out of your skull you're willing to hang out with an east-side kid.

Today, the east side sparkled under a high blue sky. The air smelled dry and good. I walked from street to street, aimlessly wandering as my heart squeezed in my chest, filled with wistful October sentimentality. I picked up a twig and gnawed on it. It tasted like wood and earth and soil. I stepped into the gutter and kicked a heavy blanket of fallen leaves, enjoying the satisfying crunch.

"Nice. You're kicking the shit out of those leaves."

I looked up. It was the pale girl. Katrina. She was lying out in the front yard of an enormous brown house and I hadn't even noticed her. Her dark hair was tied back in a ponytail and in the full, glowing light of day she was so pretty that I had trouble looking directly at her. I looked down and gave an extravagant, NFL placekicker–style kick that really sent the leafy motherfuckers flying.

"Whoa, buddy. What did they ever do to you?"

"I take my pleasures where I can."

"Oh yeah?"

Katrina sat forward, lowering an open textbook across her lap as she studied me. Taking this as an invitation, I stepped out of the gutter and walked onto her lawn, trying to seem as confidant and non-idiotic as possible. I knew I was a tall, gawky high school dude with untamable hair, but maybe she was into that type of guy.

I looked past her at the big brown house. It was ugly as hell.

"You live in Hickson?"

"Yeah," Katrina said. "This year, anyhow. I thought it'd be cool to get off-campus and live like, you know, a regular human being."

"So basically you're here for the cheap rent."

"Pretty much."

I hooked my thumbs into my pockets and squinted up at the sky. Somebody in the neighborhood was going at it with a leaf blower.

"What do you think so far?"

"Of Hickson?"

I nodded.

"Well, I'd say it's astonishingly dull so far. Astonishingly."

"Oh yeah," I said. "We've got that down pat."

Katrina closed her textbook. Environmental Philosophy. It had a desperate-looking polar bear on the cover, swimming in the ocean with no chunks of ice in sight.

"You feel like going for a drive?"

"Okay," I said. "As long as you don't take advantage of me."

Katrina laughed. She swung her pale legs out of the Adirondack chair and leapt to her feet, slipping on a pair of flip-flops laid out in the grass.

"I can't make that sort of promise, Mack-Attack."

———

We took Katrina's car. She drove recklessly and it gave me an enormous erection with every screeching turn in the road. She had a black VW Bug with skull-and-crossbones decals slapped on the doors. Her brothers were both gearheads, she shouted above the windy roar pouring in through the car's open windows, and they'd given the Bug "serious fucking balls," which meant we were able to get up to a hundred miles an hour on the straight stretches of highway, the car rattling around us like a space capsule reentering the earth's atmosphere.

"What about deer?" I hollered, shifting in my seat as I tried to hide, or at least alleviate, my hard-on.

"Deer can't go this fast," Katrina hollered back.

I sat back and enjoyed the wind as it pummeled my body and forced tears into my eyes. Hickson kids liked to tool around the local highways but I'd never seen anybody haul ass like this, much less while wearing flip-flops and black toenail polish and smoking Camel Blues.

A lumber truck appeared up ahead in our lane. Katrina screamed and jammed the gas pedal to the floor. Somehow the Bug gained even more steam, rattling cataclysmically, and we passed the lumber truck as if it were a woolly mammoth or some other dumpy prehistoric creature.

Goddamn, I liked this girl.

———————

We drove for an hour, winding our way around until I no longer recognized where we were. Trees blurred past the Bug's windows like the background scenery you'd see in an old-timey movie, their autumn leaves a mash-up of canary yellows and russet browns. When we passed the occasional field it was like coming up for air, and the blue sky seemed impossibly enormous.

At dusk, Katrina turned off whatever godforsaken highway we were driving on and into a pasture's access driveway. She didn't slow down to do this. She just flicked the steering wheel, jammed the brake pedal to the floor, and laughed manically as the car fishtailed ninety degrees before plowing to a stop, spraying dirt into the air.

A thoughtful silence followed. I registered that we were still alive and had stopped moving altogether. My shoulder ached from the dozens of collisions it had enjoyed with the passenger door, not to mention the cutting press of the seat belt. Across from us a bunch of Holsteins were grazing in the pasture, hunting half-heatedly through the drought-blighted grass for something enjoyable to chew on. Compared to the objects we'd been roaring past, they appeared almost stationary, like spotted hay bales.

Katrina unbuckled her seat belt. "Shit, that was fun."

"Yes," I said, staring ahead at the nearest cow. "Vroom."

Katrina sat forward and reached across my lap. Luckily, my hard-on had disappeared a few miles back and we avoided having an awkward discussion, at least for the moment. She popped open the glove box and fumbled around in what appeared to be a mass of paper trash. She smelled like ladies' deodorant mixed with cigarette smoke.

"Ahhh. There you are, baby."

The glove box trash dumped out on my feet as Katrina drew out a fifth of golden liquor and held it up between us, her smile as curved as a farmer's scythe. I unbuckled my seat belt and focused on the bottle, trying to ignore how close our bodies were.

She gave the bottle a happy shake. "This here is brandy."

"You keep brandy in your glove box? Are you an eighty-year-old British dude?"

"I wish. Those guys fucking rock."

Katrina took a pull from the fifth and handed the bottle to me. I took a healthy swig and my toes unclenched from their death curl inside my shoes. Katrina's seat creaked as she reclined. The Bug's interior was so small it felt like we'd shoved ourselves into an escape pod and crash-landed on a dusty, backwater planet.

I took another drink and handed the bottle back to Katrina. You could hear the car's engine clicking as it cooled, as well as the hordes of crickets and grasshoppers buzzing in abandon. Past the field and above a distant tree line the sun had started to set, turning the entire horizon golden.

"So. Katrina. What are you majoring in?"

"Art and business."

"You're a double threat."

"I'd like to own my own art gallery someday. Tour the world, buy beautiful shit. Then sell it for twice what I paid for it."

Katrina took another swig of brandy. I waited for her to pass the bottle but she kept it flat against her stomach. A cow lowed at us from the pasture, sounding confused. The Holsteins had given up grazing and had hunkered down in ones and twos.

"Don't cows go in at night? They sleep in a barn, right?"

"Yeah," I said. "I guess."

"That'd be nice. Being a cow, sleeping with all your cow pals around you, warm and safe while the wind howls outside. I'd like that."

"Huh," I said, imagining. It did sound nice.

Katrina took a nip from the bottle. "You like working at the hardware store, Mack?"

"It's okay. Kind of boring."

"I bet. I worked at Target in high school. I was a cashier."

"Really?"

"Every day was the same fucking thing. A bunch of saps buying the same old crap. Beep, beep, beep. Everybody staring at my mascara, my nose piercing. The old ladies acting like I'd gobble them up."

"Ha. I'd like to see you in those khakis."

Katrina turned and looked at me. "It was better than hanging around my house, trust me. My stepdad can get pretty grabby when Mom's not around."

"Jesus."

"Yeah, he's a real snake in the grass. That dude's got my mom wrapped around his little finger, though. I think he's a sociopath."

"Really?"

"Not the murder-spree kind, though. More like the

manipulative man-slut kind." Katrina leaned in and I could smell the brandy on her breath. "What about you, Mack? Are you a snake in the grass?"

I didn't answer. The brandy was warming my cheeks and the sun was almost halfway beneath the horizon. Everything was so beautiful.

"Shit, I don't know," Katrina said, sitting back and taking another long swig. "I guess I'm becoming … untethered. I sit in class and can't focus on anything. I feel like a helium balloon after it's been released by some chubby kid at the state fair. My brain rising and rising and rising."

"Life will make you crazy," I agreed. "No way around that."

"There isn't?"

"Not if you're paying attention."

"Well … shit."

"Yep."

Katrina handed me the brandy. I took another nip and returned the bottle. A gust of wind rustled the loose paper on the car's floor and carried the smell of wood smoke.

"I blame my mother. She's a vegetarian and made us all vegetarians, too. I probably didn't get enough iron during crucial developmental phases."

"Is she as pretty as you?"

"Prettier." A tiny smile hooked the corner of Katrina's mouth. "Why, Mack? You sweet on me?"

I closed my eyes and let the sunset burn itself into my brain. Everything turned red then gold.

"Sweet," I said, "as honey pie."

Katrina slapped my arm, sloshing brandy onto the sleeve of my T-shirt. "See? Fucking snake."

"I am not a snake, madam," I said. "I'm totally warm-blooded."

"Yeah right. You're a youngin' snake, Mack. A snake in training. I bet you're thinking about sexing me up right now. You'd probably love to turn me into your little fuck doll, wouldn't you?"

The golden light behind my eyelids turned a spotty purple. I rubbed my eyes and turned to look at Katrina. I wondered if she had some kind of mental disorder or if this fuck-doll talk was just her friendly way of passing the time. It occurred to me that she probably had her own dark shit going on. She was voluntarily hanging out with me, after all. That couldn't be a healthy sign.

A cow lowed in the field.

A second cow lowed back from a point farther away.

"Well, I don't think he's coming," Katrina said, taking a final pull from the bottle and emptying it. "Old Mac-Donald isn't taking his cows back home tonight. He's probably sitting with Ma and Junior at the kitchen table right now, enjoying an overcooked pork chop doused in cream of mushroom soup."

She capped the bottle and tossed it over her shoulder. I leaned forward, studying the cows in their darkening field.

"It's a nice evening," I said. "He probably leaves them out on nights like this."

"Like camping, but for cows."

"Why not? The cows like to see the stars, too."

A grasshopper flew up and landed on the windshield. The insect and I studied each other through the glass while Katrina shifted in her seat and groaned.

"Oh man. I think you're going to have to drive us back to town, Mack-Attack. I'm done tuckered."

She burped and I laughed.

The grasshopper flew away.

As soon as I pulled us out onto the road, Katrina slumped against the passenger window and fell asleep. She made little snoring noises, cartoonish high whistlings that sounded like a child pretending to be asleep. It took me a half-hour to find a road I recognized and another twenty minutes before I was certain I'd pointed us in the right direction. Along the way we passed through a small Amish area that was pitch black except for the Bug's headlights and the eerily beautiful kerosene lantern light that shone from the sprawling homes of the Amish themselves. I shook Katrina's shoulder so she could see the houses and she asked me if she was dreaming. I told her yes, she was, and let her fall back asleep.

The History Test

The siege continued and Mom kept chugging along. By the start of my freshman year of high school our family had grown used to how thin she was, how little she could eat with her reduced stomach, and how determined she was not only to keep on living but to participate in the world. On good days, she'd have one of us fill up R_2O_2 from the main oxygen tank and carry it out to the van for her and then she'd drive into Thorndale by herself to go shopping.

Mom was five-nine. As her weight dipped below one hundred pounds, then below ninety, her face hollowed out and her bones rose up from beneath her skin. When you hugged her you had to be careful (she cracked ribs frequently, sometimes just from coughing hard). When I hugged her, I'd feel the knobby ridge of her spine with my fingers. It reminded me of the outline of a mountain chain, or the armored plating of a small, vegetarian dinosaur.

Women joked with my mother about how they wished they could transfer some of their fat onto her and men treated her with exaggerated courtesy, holding doors and carrying anything that needed carrying. When you went out around town with her, you could feel people staring, startled by her thinness, by the fact she was still among the living. Mom didn't mind—I think she felt that it was far better to be stared at, to be seen, than to be tucked away in a hospice with more privacy than anyone could possibly want.

———

In November, I got a call from Dad during my lunch hour. He said he was taking Mom to the hospital because she was having trouble breathing. More trouble than usual, he meant. My grandparents were going to pick up Haylee and he thought it might be a good idea if I also left school early and rode with them to the hospital.

The first thing I thought about was my American history class.

"I have a test next period," I told him. "A big history test."

"You do?"

"Yeah."

Dad didn't say anything. I thought about all the long years of siege, all the false alarms and minor incidents.

"Is it okay if I take the test first and then show up? Sam's grandma can take me."

I saw Dad standing in the living room with his phone to his ear, frowning.

"Sure, Mack. That's fine. We'll meet you at the hospital."

"Cool. I'll get there as soon as I can."

I took my test and then dutifully rode with Sam's grandmother to Thorndale. At the hospital, I found my father sitting with Haylee and Grandpa and Grandma Hedley in the waiting room. They all looked worn out, blasted. They told us Mom had been sedated and put on an artificial respirator. She couldn't breathe on her own anymore.

I'd missed her by an hour.

A Slow Afternoon at
Hickson Hardware

So you went on a drive?"

"Yes."

"With her? That hot college chick from Lisa Sorenson's party?"

"Vroom vroom, baby."

"And you drank... brandy?"

"Yes."

"And you watched the sun set behind a field of cows. A beautiful, romantic sunset."

"Yes, Sam. We did."

"And you didn't put the moves on her?"

"Well—"

"Damn it, Mack. That was your shot. Your one shot at the big time."

"I didn't really see an opening—"

"And you fucked it up. You fucked it up and now she

probably thinks you're solid best friend material. You will now be BFFs."

"I don't think you should be behind the counter. What if Big Greg checks in? That's his stool you're sitting on. He loves that stool."

"Big Greg? That's what you're worrying about right now?"

"He can get mad, dude."

"No he can't."

"He yelled at this guy for returning a ladder. He'd already seen him using it to trim branches in his front yard."

"Wow."

"And then he pummeled him with both fists, Incredible Hulk-style."

"That didn't happen."

"And then he bellowed. He bellowed so loud Mr. Ladder's head exploded in a spray of meaty fragments. I had to use the wet mop and tons of bleach after that one. You wouldn't believe how much fluid the human body actually contains."

"I bet I would."

"Ha ha."

"Jesus, Mack. Do you want to be a virgin forever?"

"Sam, it's not like she's dead."

"Unless you killed her. Did you kill her, Mack? Is this really what we're talking about here? A country drive gone horribly wrong? Did you pitch her down a well? Chuck her into a bottomless sinkhole?"

"I'm laying a foundation here. It takes time."

"A foundation of death."

"What time is it, anyway? I think we've entered some kind of shadowland where the laws of time no longer apply. Purgatory."

"Her nose is pierced, man. I hear those girls are crazy in the sack."

"Why? Some kind of metal-poisoning thing?"

"Metal poisoning?"

"Metals can poison people. They seep into your blood."

"Right. Whatever. The point is—"

"Sam, I know what I'm doing here. She's a headstrong little pony and is going to take some rustling."

"That's your cowboy accent? You sound like a stroke victim."

"You're just jealous I get all the ladies."

"Wow, Mack. You went on a car ride with a girl who fell asleep. You're like a god of carnality walking amongst us mere mortals."

"I wish somebody would stop in and buy something. Just one goddamn customer."

"I thought you hated customers."

"I do."

"But without them, you're nothing. You're useless. Just a guy sitting behind a counter watching your life tick by."

"One rake. That's all. I'd just like to sell one motherfucking, ass-poking rake."

"Ass-poking?"

"It's October. People need to rake their lawns. This isn't some crazy hardware store dream, right?"

"Not as crazy as you getting it on with that goth chick."

"That dream is beautiful, Sam. Not crazy."

"If you say so."

"C'mon, people. One rake. We can do this shit."

The Graveyard

Hickson's graveyard sits on a peninsula that juts out into a polluted body of water called Baker's Lake. The graveyard's first plots were planted along the outer edges of the peninsula, with subsequent generations of dead spiraling ever inward.

The edges of the peninsula have slowly eroded over time. A few years back, we had a big spring flood that swamped everything. Later that same summer, a fisherman on Baker's Lake reeled in what he thought was a whopper of a fish but turned out to be the rib cage of a four-year-old boy.

The boy had been dead for over a hundred years.

Company

Two days after my terrifying and erotic country drive with Katrina, I came home from work to find all the lights on and jazz music coming from the kitchen. The living room had been tidied up, the hardwood floor mopped and waxed to a glossy sheen. After years of my father's laissez-faire approach to housekeeping, the effect of this domestic glow was so disorienting I checked the framed family photos on the wall to make sure I'd entered the right house.

"Mack, is that you?"

I stuck my head through the kitchen doorway.

"There he is. There's my guy."

Dad beamed at me from the stove. He was wearing a white chef's apron and his nice sweater. His round eyeglasses were fogged from stove heat.

"Hey Dad. What's up?"

"Dinner, buddy boy. That's what's up."

"You're cranking the jazz, huh?"

"We're having spicy shrimp stir-fry."

"Uh oh."

Dad laughed and wiped his hands on his apron. "C'mon, it'll be great. I got a foolproof recipe from the Internet. It got sixty-eight five-star reviews."

"Okay..."

"And I bought Thai beer. It'll be like we're eating out."

I glanced around the kitchen, noting the smell of rice pouring out of the rice cooker and the surprisingly clean counters, which were usually cluttered with dirty dishes and mangled bits of vegetable during Dad's stir-fry process. The kitchen table was covered in the good white tablecloth, had a small cattails-and-cheatgrass centerpiece, and had been set with four plates.

"We're having company, Mack. I invited a friend from work to eat with us."

My chin snapped upward. The Druneswalds weren't the kind of people that had guests over for dinner—we settled for managing to feed ourselves and called it good. Sometimes Sam showed up and ate with us, but that was only on pizza Fridays.

"Her name is Bonnie. She's the new receptionist."

"The new receptionist?"

"She's a real sweet lady. You'll like her, Mack."

Dad had turned sweaty and pale, all friendly chutzpah evaporated. I felt both sorry for him and as if I were about to puke on the heavily waxed floor. A tight, sour knot was forming in my stomach, not unlike the feeling you get after being kicked in the balls. I could only imagine this Bonnie, this office temptress.

"Does Haylee know?"

Dad took off his fogged glasses and wiped them on his apron.

"Yes."

"How'd that go?"

"Not great. I was hoping you'd go up and talk to her. I want Bonnie to feel welcome, Mack. I want everybody at the table."

I swallowed, trying to wrap my mind around this request.

"You can have the rest of the beer," Dad said in a flat voice. "Once dinner is over, you can have the rest of the Thai beer for yourself. I got a twelve pack."

Veggies sizzled in the wok. Dad fluffed the stir-fry with a spatula and I rubbed my eyes. Was all this actually happening? Dad was trying to bribe me with Thai beer? Dad had a new girlfriend?

"How long have you been seeing each other?"

"Two weeks," Dad said, looking back at me from over his shoulder. "Two pretty good weeks."

"Well," I said. "Shit."

I left the kitchen and went upstairs, my feet dragging beneath me. As I opened my bedroom door, I heard knocking on the front door downstairs. The jazz music faded away. I pictured Dad hoofing it to the entryway, no doubt wiping his sweaty hands on his chef's apron, wondering how his hair looked while a stranger stood on our front steps, waiting to be let in.

I closed my bedroom door, stubbed my toe on a stack of books, and lay down on my bed. Lying there, hands laced beneath my head as I studied the glow-in-the-dark star sticker constellation on my ceiling, I had three epiphanies in rapid order:

1. Mom was really dead, and she was not coming back. Not ever.
2. This Bonnie tramp was most likely the first real action my father had gotten in a crazy long time.
3. Free beer was free beer.

Dad called Haylee and me downstairs. I got out of bed, slapped my cheeks, and went into the hallway. I placed my ear against my sister's bedroom door and considered my best plan of attack.

"Go away."

I didn't move.

"I can hear you breathing, doofus. You sound like a big fat stalker."

I rapped gently on her door.

"Hayyy-leee," I whispered. "It's me. The dinner fairy."

"I said go away."

"Why? I've come to whisk you away to a magical land of shrimp stir-fry. Please, take my hand and I shall lead you."

"No. I'm not going down there. Not until his slutty goes home."

"Hayyy-leee. Slutty is a harsh word, Hayyy-leee."

"You're not funny, dork, and I'm not going down there."

The sound of banging came from the kitchen. Spatula-on-wok violence.

"What if, Ms. Haylee Katherine Druneswald, I told you I have been authorized to slip you one—no, two—fancy Thai beers and look the other way? Would that change your mind?"

"No. I don't even like beer."

I leaned harder against the door.

"You don't like beer? Really?"

"No. It's disgusting."

"What if I drive you to the mall?"

A pause. Tentative movement on the other side of the door.

"Really? When?"

"Whenever you want, little lady. The Olds shall be your chariot."

I stepped back as my sister opened her door and eyed me warily, looking particularly elfish with her hair tucked back behind her pointy ears.

"You swear?"

"Cross my goddamn heart."

———

Dad's new lady wasn't the salacious office vixen I'd imagined. Bonnie turned out to be a thick, bouncy gal in her mid-forties who smiled nervously as she surveyed our freshly waxed kitchen. She had brown curly hair, laugh lines around her eyes, and a polite giggle she pulled out whenever Dad made one his lame Dad jokes. Honestly, with her round face and crinkly button nose, she reminded me of a friendly lady hobbit, only taller, and that alone made it hard to dislike her.

Haylee and I sat at our usual places at the table, across from each other, while Dad had moved to my right and placed Bonnie to my left. I wondered if this was savvy arrangement on Dad's part—sitting in Mom's spot himself and thereby heading off any seating arrangement drama—or if he'd finally figured out it'd be easier to sit closer to the stove if he was the one cooking.

Two fancy new ceramic serving bowls, one filled with vegetables and shrimp, the other with white rice, had been placed on the table. Haylee slouched in her seat, touching nothing as the rest of us served ourselves. "We don't say grace," she announced, crossing her arms and glaring at our guest.

"That's fine by me," Bonnie said. "Quicker to chowing down, right?"

Dad chuckled and Haylee gave him the old Death Stare. "Where's Chompy?" she asked.

"I put him in his kennel," Dad said, stabbing a shrimp with his fork. "I thought it might be nice to have one meal without being chewed on."

"Good idea," I said, nodding. "I don't think Bonnie wants her feet molested while she's eating spicy shrimp stir-fry."

Haylee scowled. "Is she allergic to dogs or something?"

"No, I love dogs. I'm not allergic to them at all. You can bring Chompy up, Peter. I don't mind."

"I do," I said, raising my hand. "Keep that bastard down there as long as you deem necessary, Pops. God knows he's earned it."

Chompy, who must have known we were talking about him, gave one sharp, impertinent bark from the basement's moldy depths.

"You hear that?" Haylee said. "He's suffering."

"No, honey," Dad said. "He's not."

"How do you know? You don't know everything. You don't know jack."

"I know something," I said, grabbing a shrimp by its tail and whipping it around. "I know I like going to the mall."

"He's like a political prisoner down there. He can probably smell dinner."

"He has his squeaky bone. He'll be fine."

"Whatever. Like you care, anyway."

Haylee stood up and her chair tipped over and clattered to the floor, making everybody flinch. "You're both traitors, you know that?" She glared at Dad and me. "Ungrateful sleezeball traitors."

Leaning on the table, she turned the full power of her Death Stare on Bonnie, who now appeared sensibly alarmed.

"Dad sits where you're sitting. Mom sat near the stove."

Bonnie blinked and looked at our father, who'd turned

pink. Haylee walked out of the kitchen and left the house through the side door, which she slammed shut.

We all waited for a moment, wondering if the show was over, before Dad apologized to Bonnie and we started eating again. Occasionally we heard a contented squeak or two, rising up from below.

The Scarecrow

I left the house after dinner and wandered around town on foot, hoping to find Haylee, but all I saw were people walking their dogs one more time before bed or sitting in their living rooms watching TV. I hovered at each bright window, drawn to the diorama-like scenes inside like a peeping moth. Oblivious to the nighttime dark outside their windows, the people of Hickson appeared happy and content. They cuddled under blankets. They drank soda. They ate popcorn from comically oversized plastic bowls.

I kept walking until I got to the outskirts of town. The houses went dark one by one as their owners turned in for the night and eventually I was walking alone through a ghost town of rustling leaves and humming streetlights. I came to a darkened house in a darkened neighborhood with an elaborately ornamented front yard. The theme was autumn and they had the hay bales, pumpkins, gourds, bagged leaves, and full-sized mounted scarecrow to prove it.

Dressed in ragged denim overalls, the scarecrow had

black button eyes, no nose, and a squiggle of thread for a mouth. His skin was a white canvas-like material through which pieces of straw stuck out in random spots, as if he were literally bursting with straw. In lieu of the farmer's straw hat, the scarecrow wore a classic gray fedora Frank Sinatra might have appreciated.

He was so cute.

So homey.

I took out my lighter, thumbed it a few times, and touched the tentative flame to the scarecrow's chin. The fabric blackened for a second before igniting in a small flame that quickly began to spread.

"Fuck you, buddy," I whispered, staring directly into the scarecrow's button eyes.

The scarecrow didn't reply. I crossed the street and stepped behind an evergreen to watch him go up in incandescent flame, the firebug overjoyed at this sudden and unexpected treat. It wasn't until the scarecrow's sackcloth body started to sag and fall away from its post that I realized what would soon remain—two wooden poles hammered together in the shape of a cross.

"Shit."

I took off my coat, prepared to rush back across the street and smother the fire, but just then a light came on inside the scarecrow's house as someone woke up.

"Shit shit shit."

A second light came on inside the house. The time of

secret lurking was over. I lowered my head and started walking briskly home, keeping to the shadows as the firebug (the stupid, stupid firebug) pleaded with me to go back and watch until the last lick of flame died out.

The Hunt

On Saturday I woke to the sound of heavy footsteps outside my bedroom. It was still pitch dark and my digital alarm clock read six a.m. I'd gotten home from the Legion only five hours before.

The knob of my bedroom door turned and the door swung open. I sat up as a shadowy figure entered the room and stood at the foot of my bed. My visitor looked around the room slowly, as if he could see everything perfectly despite the dark. I wondered where I'd put my old pocket knife and wondered if I had the balls needed to stab a vicious intruder.

"Hey Mack. You awake?"

I reached over to my nightstand and clicked on the lamp. It was Grandpa Hedley, dressed in army boots, canvas army pants, and a blaze-orange jacket. He winced at the sudden light and shielded his eyes.

"Hey kid. Morning."

"Morning."

Grandpa Hedley surveyed my room again, frowning.

"Awful messy around here. Why do you have so many god-damn books?"

"Is that why you broke into our house at six in the morning? To talk about my personal library?"

"No," my grandfather said, scratching his stomach. "I thought we could go hunting today. Bag us some birds."

"Birds?"

"That's right. Pheasant season starts today. Thought we'd head up to Elroy County and try our luck."

"You want to go hunting? We haven't been since—"

"Sure. Thought we'd bring your mutt with us. Let him stretch his legs."

I rubbed my face in my hands. "You want to take Chompy…hunting?"

"Sure. Looks like a hunting dog to me."

I laughed, trying to picture this. Chompy in nature. Chompy gnawing on every tree in sight. Chompy lunging after squirrels.

"Get dressed, kid. I'll meet you downstairs. I already put the coffee on."

Grandpa Hedley shuffled into the hallway and started down the stairs.

"Fuck," I said aloud. "Why not?"

I slid out of bed and kicked around the clothes piled on the floor, seeking out the warmest options. I dressed slowly, my sleep-numbed brain focusing on one item at a time. By the time I made it downstairs, the whole first floor smelled like coffee. Grandpa Hedley was sitting at our table, leafing through the week's collection of bills and mail order catalogues.

After coffee, we woke the beast and released him from his basement kennel. Chompy scarfed his breakfast and happily followed us out to Grandpa's truck, where he hopped into the cab's back seat like this was something we did all the time, curling up against a plastic cooler and two compound bow cases.

"We're loaded up, huh?"

"Here," Grandpa Hedley said, reaching into the back seat and pulling out a blaze-orange coat that matched his own. "Brought one for you."

We drove north for an hour and crossed into Elroy County, stopping for breakfast at a fast food drive-thru and buying our hunting licenses at a gas station. Grandpa paid for everything, generous as a king, and we listened to country music as we rolled along, Chompy sleeping soundly in the back seat, his hind legs occasionally twitching as he ran through his dreams.

The landscape gradually changed from wooded hills to flat plains and corn fields. Grandpa studied the terrain carefully, driving with one hand hanging loosely on the truck's steering wheel. We saw a few other hunters already out, walking ditches and field edges in groups of three or four, studying the ground carefully. Eventually, when we came to a field that looked the same as every other harvested field, Grandpa pulled the truck over into the ditch and parked it on the ditch floor. Chompy stood up in the back seat and stuck his face between ours, panting happily.

"This looks good a place as any," Grandpa Hedley said. "What do you think?"

I peered through the windshield. "Yep. Looks like a field to me."

Grandpa Hedley nodded as if this wasn't a smart-ass thing for me to say and looked out his window.

"I know the guy who owns this field. Hell, he owns almost every field in this part of the state."

"You do?"

"Yes, sir. We served together."

"No shit?"

"He's an ornery bastard, but he won't mind us hunting his field. I saved him from getting stabbed by a whore once in Saigon. She came at him with a switchblade after he took up with her sister."

"Whoa."

Grandpa popped his door open and unbuckled his seat belt. "Even whores get jealous, Mack."

We got out and released Chompy, who dropped silently to the ground and ran to the edge of the field, where he lifted his leg and peed. I stood beside my grandfather in front of the truck and followed his gaze across the field.

"The birds are out here, Mack. I can feel them."

I glanced at Chompy, who hadn't bolted straight off as I'd expected but sat beside my grandfather in eerie obedience. I blew into my hands. A chilly fall day with a slight, moaning wind and no clouds. A day for hunting.

———

We worked the edge of the field. I'd never hunted pheasant before, only deer, but I knew pheasants liked to feed in the morning, doze in tall weeds during midday, and come out again near dusk. They liked gravel because the grit helped them digest their food and they were easiest to shoot if you flushed them from cover and they decided to fly, which gave you a big, flapping target.

Grandpa Hedley worked four rows deep into the field while I walked its edge and watched the tall ditch grass. Chompy, who was just fucking full of surprises today, was running twenty yards ahead of us, zigzagging along as if he'd been an English squire's hunting dog in a prior life, methodically scenting both the field and the ditch as his furry black tail wagged happily. I walked with my bow lowered at my side, a carbon arrow notched and at the ready. Grandpa Hedley preferred bow hunting to rifles or shotguns because he thought bow hunting was more difficult and required more skill—my grandfather was a caveman at heart, a real Beowulf-type warrior. Part of me hoped we wouldn't find anything, not one damn bird, and another part wanted to slay a dozen of the unlucky and cook up a feast right there in the woods.

We walked for about a half hour, nobody speaking as we eyed the ground, until finally Chompy stopped, coiled on his haunches, and leapt into a dense patch of cornstalks, barking with a hellhound's fury.

A blur of pheasant darted from the cornstalks, through the field's last few rows, and into the ditch. I raised my bow and drew a bead on a bird, drawing back the arrow. I hoped the bird would take flight but it stayed low, moving fast and jittery. I aimed for a point just ahead of its trajectory and loosed my arrow.

The arrow whistled through the air and planted into the ground. The bird juked around it and kept running.

I lowered my bow. The bird grew smaller and disappeared into the weeds.

"Fuck me."

Chompy burst out of the field, furry head rotating. He sniffed the air and looked at me, his eyes full of reproach.

"What? It was fast, you dick."

Chompy barked and sniffed the ground, tail wagging as he found the scent and started up the ditch. Grandpa Hedley came tromping out of the field, his bow raised and his eyes on the dog.

"Ran off on you?"

"Yeah. I missed."

Grandpa Hedley stared at the dog. He didn't look mad or disappointed. Just intense.

"It's all right, letting the first one go. Lets the other ones know we mean business."

I walked to the arrow and pulled it out of the ground. I rubbed dirt off the tip.

"You think so?"

"Sure. More sporting this way."

Chompy, who'd disappeared into the weedy yonder, popped back out and barked at us, urging us on.

"Okay, asshole. We get it."

Grandpa Hedley laughed, which was rare for him. The

old man often grinned cannily, or smiled knowingly, but he wasn't a big laugh-out-loud sort of guy. We started up the ditch, now walking side-by-side as we followed the dog through the weeds.

"You know, back in Nam we had a rifleman in our platoon who could drink half a bottle of whiskey and still shoot the tits off a mouse," Grandpa Hedley said. "Reggie Henderson, his name was. Yes, sir, Old Reggie was funny as hell. You played poker with him and he'd have everybody busting a gut by the third hand. He had a way of telling a story that could draw you in and then, right when you thought you knew what the punch line was, he'd turn the whole thing upside down."

"Huh. He sounds cool."

Grandpa nodded, his eyes still fixed on the weeds in front us. I'd gotten a burr in my sock but didn't want to stop and take it out during the story. I could feel the burr scraping against my ankle, hungry for a taste.

"Funny guy, but Reggie did have a temper. I think something real bad happened to him once and he never let it go. You could hear it in his voice sometimes. Late at night, when we'd all stayed up one round too long, he'd get a nasty edge that made his jokes sound mean."

Grandpa scratched his nose with the sleeve of his coat.

"One day, when we were out on patrol, a little Vietnamese kid popped out of the weeds and ran in front of our squad. Not at our squad, mind you, but in front of it, about fifty yards off. The kid couldn't have been more than five years old and was skinny as a goddamn mule.

"Reggie raised his rifle and sighted the kid. The rest of us thought Reggie was joking, but he fired. One shot and the kid dropped like he'd been knocked on the head with a mallet. Reggie turned and looked at us. 'How'd y'all like that one?' he said and then winked like the whole thing was a big joke. Our staff sergeant, who'd been standing beside me the whole time, pulled out his pistol and shot Reggie right between the eyes, like the whole thing was a Western on TV."

Grandpa wet his lips. A whippoorwill called out from the rows of broken corn stalks and we started walking again, following the dog and listening to the wind rustle the high grass. Finally Chompy, who must have lost the bird's scent, bounded out of the ditch and ran back down the road to rejoin us. Grandpa Hedley scratched the dog behind the ears, telling him he was a good boy.

"What do you think Reggie couldn't let go of?" I asked. Chompy rolled onto his back, showing us his white belly.

"Hell if I know, Mack. But it didn't really matter, did it? Not after Reggie was lying in that field with a bullet between his eyes."

I knelt and scratched the beast, picturing a skinny little kid running across the field, scared as hell and about to die.

"What about your staff sergeant? Did he get court marshaled for shooting Reggie?"

"Shit no. It was Vietnam, kid. We took fire the next day and Sarge bought the farm, too."

I stood up and looked at my grandfather. I saw the canny glint in his eye and I realized he suspected me of ... something. Maybe he thought I was the county firebug, maybe he just thought I'd been stepping out in other unseemly ways. Maybe he could just sense all the crazy jumping beans inside my head and thought he could freak me out before I went down The Wrong Path. He'd already gotten me a second job on the weekends—the time for making trouble—and he was always studying me like I was one of his bonsai trees. Maybe he thought he could be both my hunting grandpa and my new mommy, all rolled into one bristly war vet package. And if Grandpa Hedley thought that ... well Jesus, he was in for a big-time case of disappointment.

A critter, unseen, rustled in the distant weeds. Chompy rolled back onto his feet and shot forward. The hunt was back on but we didn't see another bird until dusk, when two beautiful ring-necks flew up on the edge of the road. Grandpa brought them down with one arrow each, smiling as they fell from the sky and Chompy ran out after them. Then we threw the dead birds in the bed of the pickup and headed for home, the dog happily snoring in the back seat while Grandpa and I watched the road in companionable silence, thinking about whatever the hell it is men think about in Ernest Hemingway stories.

The Attic

After Grandpa Hedley dropped me off at home, I worked my usual Saturday evening shift at the Legion. The crowd was a sparse collection of old men and divorced ladies, most of them with skin resembling teriyaki beef jerky, but Ox Haggerton wasn't one of them. Actually, the old coot hadn't returned to the bar once since I'd torched his woodpile. Folks said he'd grown even stranger and more isolated since the fire at his place and had taken to driving around the county day and night without stopping to speak to anyone or having an apparent destination.

After we closed the bar, I drove back to town. The night was clear and crisp with plenty of stars and I didn't feel like going home. I let the steering wheel guide me and after some slow drifting, including one close call with a parked car, I found the Oldsmobile leading me to Katrina's rental house and parking itself across the street, stakeout-style. It was past midnight but I was still surprised to see the big house dark on all levels. Didn't college students live here? Was it not Saturday night?

I leaned back into the crushed velour depths of the Oldsmobile's front seat. I closed my eyes and must have dozed off for a while, because the next thing I knew somebody was tapping on my window and I was pitching forward against my seat belt, startled as shit.

A girl laughed. It was Katrina, a pale specter in the streetlight.

I rolled down my window.

"Hey," I said. "What's up?"

Katrina stuck her hands into her jacket pockets and gave me the once-over. "You tell me, buddy. You drunk parking?"

"Nope. I'm sober as a Mormon."

Katrina snorted. "Well, I'm not. I was just at the worst party, like, ever."

"Yeah?"

"Some frat thing in Thorndale." Katrina winced and scrunched up her nose. "I let my roommates drag me to it and ended up fending off all sorts of baseball cap lechery while my roomies vanished on me. It was like going to a party with the three ghosts of unwanted pregnancy future. I took off without them. They can find their own greasy ride home."

She flapped her jacket pockets. "Anyway. You stalking me or what?"

I set my hands on the steering wheel. "I let my car guide me on my way home from the Legion and it led me here, to your darkened door. Then I conked out."

Katrina looked back at her house. "My door is darkened, isn't it? Fuck. It's downright creepy."

"Have you had the basement fumigated for giant spiders, or vampires? Also, the attic. Have you checked the attic for murderous hobos?"

Katrina shivered. "I was going to have it checked out but, you know, classes started."

"Maybe you should have a friend investigate it with you. Someone who can watch your back."

Katrina nodded, making a serious face. She didn't seem drunk. "You know, that might be a good idea. Why don't you come in and lend a hand?"

"I could find time in my schedule," I said, opening my door. "We should have a cocktail first, though. It'll help with our bravery."

———

Katrina's rental house appeared even bigger on the inside. All high tin ceilings, wood trim, and lead-framed windows, it had a basement as well as three complete aboveground stories and an attic. It must have been the house of a Hickson lumber baron once, or a big-time fur trapper. No matter how many lights Katrina flipped on, I had the strange sensation that within the house there existed some spaces light could not, or would not, reach.

We gravitated to the kitchen. Katrina fixed us drinks while I searched for a flashlight and any other ghost hunting equipment we might need. I found a battery-operated plastic lantern, a can of bug spray, and a wooden tenderizing mallet that had a reassuring heft to it. I spread everything on the table and considered the possibilities. Katrina handed me a glass tumbler filled with ice and a murky concoction she'd garnished with a maraschino cherry.

"It's an Old Fashioned."

I took a sip. Little sparks popped along my tongue. I tasted bourbon, sweet orange, and a stunning Other.

"Wow. This is the perfect concoction to drink before venturing off to face supernatural foes."

We clinked glasses and drank. The house was so cold it felt as if we'd stumbled into an ancient Victorian tomb with a well-stocked liquor cabinet.

"I like this place," I said. "It's unsettling."

Katrina wiped her mouth. "I like it too, but sometimes I think I might not be goth enough for it. You know, like I'm a poser and this shit is the real deal."

"Like H.P. Lovecraft might be buried beneath it. Waiting to rise once again when summoned by the great space demons."

Katrina tucked a strand of hair behind her ear and stepped forward. She lifted onto her tiptoes, held my gaze for a moment, and kissed me. Her lips tasted like sweet orange.

"You've read Lovecraft?" she asked.

I licked my lips. This I had not expected. "Yes I have. I love Lovecraft."

"That's kind of hot, Mack. I love old H.P. I love ancient Elder gods and weird shit from outer space."

"Lonely bookish male scientists, slowly going mad while investigating areas in rural New England."

Katrina slapped my arm. "Exactly. I love shit like that."

I nodded. My lips were still tingling and this girl liked

her Lovecraft. The universe did indeed contain a multitude of possibilities.

"You taste good, Katrina."

"Yeah, I know." Katrina picked up the plastic lantern from the table and turned it on. "Where should we start first: the basement or the attic?"

"Basement. That way, nothing can sneak up on us from below while we're searching the rest of the house."

"Yeah, dude. I like the way you think."

We descended the basement stairs and I said a silent prayer to the gods of good luck, ghost hunting, and eroticism. I'd left the bug spray on the kitchen table but had taken the wooden mallet for good luck. Katrina led the way with the lantern and refused to turn on any additional lights, not wanting to scare the haunts away.

The basement was filled with junk. Previous tenants had ditched whatever the hell they'd felt like ditching—A/C units, box fans, floor lamps, moldy rugs, wicker chairs, library books, old *Penthouses*, plastic tubs stuffed with clothes, boxes full of random mechanical stuff, an enormous CRT monitor, antifreeze, car oil—and the result was a maze of shit nobody would ever need to use again, not in a hundred years, not if there was a goddamn zombie apocalypse. The layered mess reminded me of my grandparents' cluttered backyard, though with one key difference: every object in the Grotto had been placed lovingly, with great forethought, while all the shit in Katrina's basement appeared to have been dumped as swiftly as possible.

We inspected the premises and decided nothing super-naturally depraved was holed up among the boxes and discarded furniture.

"It's the Basement of Misfit Crap," I said.

"I know, right? It's sad down here, but Charlie doesn't care."

"Your landlord?"

"Yeah. He's lazy as hell. Check out the way back room, though."

Katrina led the way through the maze of junk and stepped through a narrow doorway I hadn't noticed before. She reached above her head and pulled on a cord, flooding the small room with light.

"Welcome to my laboratory, Mack-Attack."

I stepped inside the way back room. It was narrow and long with a work bench lining the entire rear wall. Unlike the rest of the basement, it was refreshingly clear of random junk. The only items in sight were a collection of tools on the bench, stacks of squared exterior plywood, and about two dozen small wooden houses lined up in a row, some finished and some still under construction. Sawdust coated the floor and the workbench, giving off a pleasant woodsy smell.

"Wow," I said, genuinely stunned. The bird houses were painted all kinds of crazy colors, everything from lemon yellow with a lime green trim to a kaleidoscopic of punchy blues, purples, and reds. I stepped closer to examine a lilac-colored house and noticed a small white shape perched inside its opening.

"What the hell?"

It was a tiny white skeleton.

The skeleton of a bird.

"You like it?"

The skeleton was held together with a fine, bendy kind of wire. Exquisitely small, the bird's bone beak was glued open, as if it was singing, and its bony wings were cocked backward. You could see the bird's tiny vertebrae, its tiny rib cage, its blade-like sternum, its tiny phalanges. It looked so fragile and small, like it was begging to be held in your hand and crushed into powder.

I felt a lump in my throat. My eyes dampened and I wondered if I was going to cry right the fuck there. The dead bird looked so … vulnerable.

"I order the skeletons from a guy online," Katrina said. "He's a weirdo, but he does good work."

I moved on to the next bird house. This one had a skeleton bird too, though its head was down and it was staring at its feet.

"It's sleeping," Katrina said. "It's a nightingale."

I went from house to house. Different colors, different skeleton birds. It was like a housing development in the bird afterlife. I counted thirteen finished birdhouses and three still under construction. I ran a hand through my hair and looked at Katrina.

"Holy fuck, these are sweet."

"You like them?"

"Hell yes."

Katrina crossed her arms. "My roommates think I'm a

freak, but the houses are sort of like my ... dark therapy, I guess."

"I have dark therapy," I said. "I write short stories. They're really weird."

"You do?"

I nodded, still mesmerized. The skeleton birds really set the houses ... off.

Katrina picked up a hacksaw, thumbed the blade, and set it down again. "Okay," she said, reaching out and yanking on the light bulb cord. "Let's keep hunting."

We went back upstairs. We preformed a sweep of the second and third floors, which were filled mostly with bedrooms. Katrina's room was downright spartan. Other than clothes, she only had a laptop, a Salvador Dalí print, and a few art books.

"You don't have much stuff, do you?"

"I don't want it. I travel light in case shit goes down."

"Like what?"

"I don't know. Bad shit."

Katrina scratched her face with her lantern hand, sending waves of light rippling across the walls. Nobody spoke as she twisted the lantern back and forth and we watched shadows move across the room.

"All right, dude," Katrina said at last. "It's time for the final, spookiest room of all."

"The attic?"

"You bet your sweet tits the attic."

The attic was accessible only via trapdoor. Tall as I was,

I still had to stand on a chair to reach the door's hook and pull down its accordion ladder.

"Gah!"

Dust poured out the attic's hatch and sifted down into the hallway. I coughed and waved it off, which only made the dust angry and churn with rage.

"Yeesh. Just stop swatting, would you?"

I calmed myself and allowed the dust to settle. Katrina raised the lantern toward the darkened hatch, her forehead furrowing. I gestured grandly up accordion stairway and smiled.

"After you, m'lady."

Katrina glanced at the tenderizing mallet in my hand. Her pale skin was extra luminous in the lantern's light and she stood balanced on the balls of her feet, as if ready to lunge in any direction at any moment.

I held the mallet out to her. "You want the smasher?"

Katrina paused, thinking. "You know, what if you're the serial killer? What if this is all an elaborate setup to get me in the attic where no one can hear me scream?"

"Do I look like a serial killer?"

"No, but that's the point, right? It's always the normal-looking ones that are really fucked up. The button-downed, polite young men with the squeaky clean hairstyles that open the door for you and help you with your groceries."

"That's a good point," I admitted. Katrina stepped closer and held the lantern to my face.

"I think you've got some kind of secret, Mr. Mack. Something you haven't told me yet. Something big."

I smiled and the firebug bumped inside my chest. "Okay," I said, raising my hands in the air. "I'll admit it. I have a crush on you."

"Hmmm," Katrina said, lowering the lantern and starting up the accordion stairs. I followed behind, careful to keep my distance. The stairs held beneath our weight and soon we were standing in a big, empty attic.

"Nothing's up here?" Katrina said, head swiveling. "Are you freaking kidding me? Nothing?"

The attic had two rectangular windows, one at each end. We looked out the front window and saw our cars parked across from each other. We looked out the other window and peered into the backyard, which was too dark to see much of anything.

Our survey complete, Katrina sat down on the attic floor and crossed her legs beneath her. "That's the problem with life, Mack-Attack. You hope for something cool, something magical and out of the ordinary, but you usually get nothing but an empty attic without even one murderous hobo in it."

I sat across from her and tapped on the floor with the mallet. The kiss in the kitchen, combined with the Old Fashioned and the ghost hunt, had warmed my blood. I felt good. At ease. It was time for an unburdening.

"You know those fires people have been talking about? The arsonist?"

Katrina's eyes widened. "Yeah?"

"That's me. I'm the firebug."

Katrina slapped her hand over her mouth. "Get the fuck out. That was you?"

I shrugged, smiling. The firebug did a little dance inside my heart, warmed by the unexpected attention.

"I started with the fires a couple of years ago, after my mom died. It's been mostly little stuff out in the country until lately, I guess. It's weird, but somehow the fires help, you know? Like it helps to destroy something. To step back and watch it all burn."

Katrina lowered her hand from her mouth and grinned, her dark eyes gleaming. "Fuck yes. I do know how that feels. I know exactly."

"You do?"

Katrina turned off the lantern and the attic went dark, lit only by a faint scrim of starlight coming in through the windows. I heard rustling and my own breathing magnified. I thought of the skeleton birds roosting in the basement, propped up by modeling wire for all eternity. Did the skeleton birds dream? Had the birds dreamt while they were alive?

"Katrina?"

The pale outline of a girl appeared amid the darkness, crawling toward me on the floor. "So," she said, arching her back and kissing my chin. "What do you say we haunt this attic ourselves, firebug?"

Football

Football is big in Balrog County. Really big. You cannot escape this fact and simply must live with it as best you can.

High school football games draw big crowds and grown men allow their moods to be altered by their outcomes. I've never been what you'd call football material but I did enjoy the games when I was little. This was because all the kids would stop watching the game after the first quarter and we'd congregate in an open corner on the visitor's side, near the concession stands. We'd run around tagging and tackling and it was kind of exciting, wondering if certain girls liked you and if you liked them. Seeing how many friends you could get to cluster around you at once.

The Fog

I wandered through the next few days like a man who'd taken opium and proceeded to wander into a thick fog. Everything around me appeared haloed, almost fuzzy, and I found myself stroking various types of fabric and marveling at their texture, at the rich variety of their weave. Not only had I finally lost my pesky virginity, but the idea that I, skinny/dorky/underemployed Mack Druneswald, had slept with a girl as beautiful as Katrina was a marvel I could barely process, something that needed to seep in over a large period of time with the additional reassurance of physical proof.

Luckily, I had one of the metal clip barrettes she'd been wearing in her hair. It had fallen out during our glorious roll-around and I'd come across it during the post-game dressing and fumbling about. I'd tucked it into my pants quickly, like a master thief, and brought it back with me to the house.

Now I kept it in the front pocket of jeans, clicking it every now and then with a goofy smile on my face.

Click-click.

Click-click.

I went on walks early in the morning and late at night. I wandered the streets of Hickson alone, fallen leaves crackling beneath my feet as I hummed Van Morrison songs and wondered what Katrina was doing at that moment. She hadn't contacted me since our attic rendezvous but she'd seemed to enjoy herself at the time, exuding none of the after-sex shame you might have expected from a sudden hookup, only a satisfied sleepiness that made her even more attractive and caused me to imagine her reclining in an actual bed, her dark hair fanned across a pillow.

I received my share of looks as I ambled around Hickson grinning like an escaped mental patient, but I didn't mind. Everything turned me on. I got hard-ons from sitting on stools, from turning up the radio in my car, from watching sitcoms on my living room couch. In fact, it got so bad I had to consciously avoid going into full-on stalker mode and kept to one iron-fast rule: I avoided the city block Katrina lived on as if it were a quarantine zone infested with vampires, rabid dogs, and bright-eyed college kids holding clipboards. I believed if she saw me passing her house she'd realize what a true loser I was and lose all interest in me immediately. Then she'd move on to someone more her type, like a rich stockbroker or a Navy SEAL.

I managed to keep our tryst secret for three days before I broke down and told Sam about it. We were at Sunburst Lanes, a bowling alley in Thorndale we liked to hang out at when the general Hickson ennui grew overwhelming. We'd already bowled two games and had started into our second pitcher of Coke as we rested up for the third game, sprawled comfortably in the lane's plastic seats.

"Damn, Mack. You've got to be kidding me."

"No, sir. I am not."

"She let you fuck her in the attic?"

"Let me? It was her idea. I would have settled for some groping. Shit. I would have settled for holding hands."

"An attic is not a very classy place to make love."

"Yeah."

"But it sounds awesome. Congrats, dude. Goodbye virginity."

I nodded and sipped my soda, not wanting to rub it in. Sam rested his hands on his plump stomach and steepled his fingers, looking more like a young Orson Welles than ever.

"Have you talked to her since?"

"Nope."

"This is a tactical stance?"

"Nope. I don't have her phone number."

"Fuck."

Three lanes down, a middle-aged woman in mom jeans picked up a 7/10 split. She was good, and she'd been making everyone else look crappy since she'd shown up a half-hour before with her pink bowling glove, sparkly pink ball, and gritty look of determination. She might have been a school bus driver or a cleaning lady, but in this glossy bowling world she was a goddamn queen.

"This must be karma," Sam said, sitting up. "Katrina must be a reward for all the crap you've gone through."

"You mean my mom?"

"Yeah, dude. Katrina is your cosmic reward for all that painful shit. For the cancer."

I pictured an enormous balance scale floating in outer space. Sitting in one pan was an oxygen tank, a hospital bed, and my mother's gravestone. Sitting in the other pan was Katrina, wearing her leather jacket and holding a bird house under one arm.

"That's insane, Sam. If anyone needed to be rewarded, it was my mom. She was the one who had cancer."

"How do you know she wasn't? She could be chillin' in heaven right now, drinking heaven margaritas by the side of the heaven pool. Katrina is, like, your side reward. Not heaven, maybe, but pretty good, right?"

I stood up. "You're getting too mystical for me, dude. Let's roll."

"You think I'm wrong?"

"No. I think you've been spending too much time watching evangelical Christian programming with your grandma."

"She likes it when I watch TV with her. She finds it comforting."

I grabbed my twelve-pounder and stepped onto the hardwood floor. Three lanes down, Mom Jeans rolled a thunderous strike and walked back calmly to the conveyor, looking up at the flashing X on the screen. I took a step back, wound up, and rolled.

For a moment it looked like a perfect bowl, a straight-on strike, but after some wobbling indecision the five pin refused to go down and remained standing, pointing like a middle-finger right back at me.

"You should take Katrina to homecoming, if you guys are such good fuck-buddies now. Parade your college girl around the school. Make all the assholes jealous."

I scratched my head, imagining the scene. "Maybe I will and maybe I will. A man can only take being called 'Drunesdick' so many times before he froths over."

"Shit," Sam said, rising from his plastic chair. "Maybe I'll go to the dance myself to see this shit."

An uneasy peace had fallen over the House of Druneswald. On Wednesday night, Dad, who'd been trying to play it cool with Bonnie, invited her over for dinner a second time. My sister appeared much calmer this time around and made it through the entire meal without going batshit crazy. But later, when I was brushing my teeth upstairs, I could hear the TV downstairs (some romantic comedy Dad and Bonnie were watching) and the noise rose up from the stairwell like an artifact from an impossibly distant, sun-blessed past, as if the previous terrible years had not happened and I could simply bound downstairs and find Mom and Dad on the couch, snuggled together beneath a quilt.

Dad said something and Bonnie giggled like a woman who'd been nibbled upon. I imagined Haylee sitting in her room and hearing this flirty giggle sifting through her door. I saw her face scrunch and her eyes flare, her jaw setting in anger. She had no clear opponent, really, and I think that just made everything worse.

The Mayor's Corner

Dear Residents of Hickson,

Unfortunately, I write with more bad news. The seasonal yard decorations of local resident Shirley Klondike were recently destroyed in what police believe to be an act of criminal arson. Not only were her decorations ruined but the resulting image created by the arson (whether intentional or not) was a burning cross, which nearly gave poor Shirley a heart attack.

Once again, I find myself infuriated by the lowlife(s) who persists in attacking the property of innocent, law-abiding citizens. The fact that they've chosen to publish a retort to this mayoral column, in this very newspaper, shows exactly how brazen they are, while the fact that they've sent the reply anonymously, with no return address, reveals their true cowardice.

For those of you who do not know Shirley personally, I can tell you she is a swell woman who takes great pride in keeping her lawn tidy and decorated in accordance with the changing seasons. She also makes a mean beer-cheese soup, as anyone who has ever attended a soup supper at the Methodist church will agree.

To the residents of this fine town, I again ask for continued vigilance until these perpetrators are caught and dealt with appropriately. If you see anything do not hesitate to call the police or myself.

Also, I would like to remind everyone that the city will be picking up yard refuse bags this Thursday, so make sure you get outside and rake that lawn!

Sincerely,

Mayor George Hedley

Popping the Question

So ... Katrina."

"Yeah?"

"Sorry I haven't called or anything. I really did have fun the other night. You know, in the attic. Also, I need your phone number."

"So that's why you've showed up on my doorstep with flowers, like we're in the 1950s? Are these jerkwad apology flowers?"

"Urrrr ... "

"Jesus, Mack. Are you sweating?"

"I ... I ... uuuhhhhhhhh ... "

"For fuck's sake, dude. What is it?"

"Well, you know. Homecoming is tomorrow night. Homecoming homecoming homecoming."

"Ah."

"Football game, boring parade. Big dance in the old gymnasium. Lots of bunting, I imagine."

"Are you high right now?"

"And a man, Katrina, a man needs a date at times like this. Someone to lean on in case he pulls a muscle."

"Are you, like, asking me to your high school homecoming dance?"

"Yes?"

"Fuck, dude."

"I know it might seem puerile—"

"I'd fucking love to go!"

"Really?"

"Shit yeah. I never went to any dances when I was in high school. I was too busy being cool and, you know…"

"Goth?"

"Right. Goth. But now, you know, I think I'll appreciate it more now. Actually enjoy the corniness of it."

"Are *you* high right now?"

"I'll get us more brandy. I'll wear my slutty black dress. And you better have a goddamn corsage when you pick me up."

"Okay. Corsage store, here I come."

"That's right. I'm a princess, Mack Druneswald. A fucking princess."

Homecoming

Homecoming week was a big deal at Hickson High and to the weirdly supportive parents of its students, many of whom stopped by the hardware store for parade float supplies. Big Greg loved homecoming too, and not only because he could sell a shitload of two-by-fours and rubber cement. He'd played football for the Hickson Wildcats and considered this period of his life a golden age, a time when men were men and the women downright magical. He'd played both offensive and defensive tackle and had been named to the All-Conference team at both positions, which was apparently a rare feat and had given him endless fodder for manly hardware store conversations.

Business was brisk all week and I also had a shitload to do at school. By the time I got off work on Friday, I was tired and not exactly excited to cram myself into a suit and tie, even if I'd gotten a night off from the Legion because of the dance. I found my sister upstairs, running around in her underwear as her bedroom stereo blasted excruciating club music. I stood at the top of the stairs, bewildered, and caught Haylee by the wrist as she darted past.

"WHAT ARE YOU DOING?"

"I'M GETTING READY FOR THE DANCE, DUR."

"TURN DOWN THE DAMN MUSIC."

"FINE. LET ME GO."

Haylee turned the music down and I retreated to my room. I lay down on my bed, hoping for some pre-dance shuteye, but found any chance I had at sleep destroyed by the skittering about of my sister as she got ready, her hair dryer roaring while Chompy, himself revved up, barked steadily at the heels of his mistress. The best I could do in lieu of sleep was cram a pillow over my face and picture Katrina naked. This was a coping mechanism I'd been using all week when faced with the choosier customers at the store, the ones who wondered why a small-town hardware store didn't have a larger selection of colored crepe paper.

I'd almost managed to drift off when I heard a rapping upon my chamber door.

"Mack."

"What?"

"Will you come out here a second?"

"Why?"

"Please?"

I groaned into my pillow and flung it to the floor. "Damn, Haylee. Can't a man get some sleep around here?"

I opened my door. A pretty girl in a wispy lilac dress was standing in the hallway, holding Mom's old digital camera. Her brown hair was carefully pinned up, revealing the magical power of her elfish ears, while the freckles on her nose stood out beneath a light sheen of sparkly powder.

"Yowza. You look real pretty, Haystack."

My sister blushed and held out Mom's camera. "Will you take my picture?"

"Sure."

I took the camera and turned on the hallway lights. Haylee stared straight ahead for the first four pictures, unsmiling, as if posing for a driver's license photo, but then Chompy jumped up and photobombed the fifth one, his big, slobbery head eating up the foreground while my sister cracked a grin.

"This one's a winner," I said, handing the camera back to her.

"Thanks. You're really going to the dance, Mack?"

"Yep."

"I didn't even know you had a girlfriend."

"We're not labeling it."

"But she's coming with you?"

"Yes."

"And she's real?"

"Ha. Her name's Katrina. She's in college."

Haylee tilted her head, squinting at me like a tiny, elfish gunslinger. Chompy barked uncertainly and grabbed my ankle in his maw, seeking toothy reassurance. Soon I would need to take a shower and ready myself.

"Who are you going with, Haystack? Some captain of industry? A fellow future big shot corporate lawyer?"

"Just Staci and Bridgette. We don't need men to validate our lives, Mack."

"So, what you're saying here is hos before bros?"

"God, you're a dork."

———————

The homecoming dance was held in our high school's gym, which was basically a raised basketball court wedged between wooden bleachers and a four-hundred-seat auditorium. The basketball court also served as a stage—enormous black velvet curtains could be pulled across the basketball hoops and wooden risers to hide them from the auditorium crowd. Every big school event was held in this multi-use space: terrible plays, boring basketball games, endless band concerts, iffy talent shows, lame pep rallies, and sniffly student memorial services.

Tonight the gym was gussied up for homecoming. The ceiling above the basketball court was filled with hundreds of silver and blue helium balloons, as if some enormous spider creature had laid its eggs there, and both the auditorium and the wooden bleachers were decorated with streamers. The hired DJ had set up a light-and-sound show, complete with a smoke machine and an enormous freestanding disco ball, and the floor was already populated by clumps of students dancing. It was a big crowd. Unlike prom, which was only open to seniors, juniors, and their dates, anybody in grades nine through twelve could attend homecoming. Also, it was only a semi-formal, which meant plenty of dudes wearing their father's ill-fitting suits and girls done up like they were going clubbing in New Jersey. The freshmen, I noticed, looked particularly terrified, choosing to hang back on the edges of the raised court as if they'd come solely to chaperone the dance themselves.

As Katrina and I stood at the edge of the auditorium, with all this pseudo-glamour spread out before us, I wondered if I'd made perhaps the greatest mistake of my spastic life. It was one thing to attend your school's lame dance alone or with another student from your school; it was quite another to see the whole freak show through the eyes of a stranger. An older, way cooler stranger.

"Wow."

"Katrina—"

"I mean, wow. Holy shitfuck."

"We can leave if you want."

"Leave?" Katrina turned to me and grabbed my hand. "No way, Mack-Attack. This is good clean fun. This is high school distilled."

"Yeah, unfortunately."

"Aw, shut up."

Katrina dragged me through the auditorium and up onto the dance floor. She danced in a funky, uninhibited way while I tried to boogie without looking too much like I'd been electrocuted, which is hard to do when you're ninety-percent elbows.

"Mack."

"What?"

"Stop grinning like that. You look like an idiot."

"Sorry."

I closed my eyes and tried to focus on the music. I was groovy, I was groovy...

Somebody hip-checked me, knocking me out of the groove. I opened my eyes, expecting one of our school's resident douche nozzles, but instead I found Haylee standing in front of me, stock still in the crowd of dancers.

"Hey," my sister shouted. "Is that her?"

I looked at Katrina. She was watching us but hadn't stopped dancing. She was wearing a little black dress that fluttered when she moved. She reminded me of a gypsy minus all the rings and bracelets.

"She's so old," Haylee shouted. "Is she twenty-one?"

"I like your dress," Katrina shouted back across the dance floor. "Lilac's a good color for you."

Haylee stared at Katrina, pursing her lips so tight they almost disappeared entirely. I had no idea what her deal was, but she definitely didn't look like someone who was enjoying a homecoming dance.

No. More like someone who was going to bomb a homecoming dance.

The fast song ended and a slower song started, some terrible heartstring of a country song that made the girls whoop and rush the dance floor. A sophomore girl grabbed Haylee by the hand and pulled her into the crowd, shouting something unintelligible. Katrina stepped closer and put her arms around my neck. I put my hands on her waist and we started slow dancing. I could feel the warmth of her hips through the fabric of her dress.

"Who was that girl?"

"That's Haylee. She's my sister."

Katrina nodded. "I like her. She seems tough."

"Oh, she's a real badger, all right."

Even though Katrina was in heels, I loomed over her shoulder with my tottering height. So this was a high school dance without the loneliness, alienation, or the terrible, cellular-level despair. This was dancing with the prettiest girl in the joint while your heart went thumpity-thump in your chest and your mouth dried out and sweat welled along your hairline, just waiting to break free and stream down your face.

"I could get used to this," I said.

"Yeah?" Katrina said. "Well, don't."

I forced myself to focus on the crowd as a steadying measure as my fellow Wildcats drifted around the dance floor. Fog drifted knee-high around the room, obscuring ankles and shoes, while the mirror ball dotted the darkness with luminous white flares. I noticed Haylee dancing at the edge of the floor with some ginger-haired dude with broad shoulders and I gave her a nod, some brotherly hey-there support, but she didn't notice me. She was frowning in concentration, the boy handling her like he was dancing with a mannequin or his favorite blow-up doll, and when the song ended my sister pulled away from him and practically sprinted out of the gym.

"Ugh," Katrina said, stepping back and scowling at the DJ. "I hate this song. Let's go sit down."

We went to sit in the auditorium. Watching the dancing

couples and clumps of dancing friends wasn't that different from taking in a basketball game or a really loosely plotted play.

"So this is it," Katrina said. "These are the days of our lives."

"You really never went to a school dance? Not once?"

Katrina shook her head. "I didn't like boys much. I thought I might be a lesbian but I kind of hated girls, too. I hated everybody except my cat, Bauhaus."

"We just got a dog. He's a lunatic."

"I liked to lie on the floor of my bedroom and pretend I was dead. I imagined what my funeral would be like and waited to see how long it would take Bauhaus to find me on the floor. He'd come up and meow in my face. If I didn't get up, he'd curl up under my chin and start purring."

"What was being dead like?"

Katrina shrugged and took out her cell phone. "Quiet, I guess."

The song changed and Katrina started texting someone. I left her and walked up to the entryway to get us punch. I'd filled one plastic cup when Sam appeared, sweating and wearing the same black suit he'd worn to my mother's funeral. It was a wee bit tighter on him now.

"Hey dude. You did show up."

"Mack, you need to come with me."

"What?"

"Just come on."

I tossed the punch back and left the cup on the table. Sam was clearly agitated, his lunky head bobbing between his shoulders, and he walked at double-time speed. He led me out of the auditorium's entryway and into the school's main hall. Couples were whispering against the wall, cozied up in corners. Sam ignored them and kept walking down the main hall, passing the principal's office and the gym's side entrance.

"What is it, Sam? Katrina's waiting for me."

"It's Haylee. She got in a fight."

"What?"

We reached a crowd of students huddled outside the girl's bathroom. You could hear a woman talking sternly on the other side of the bathroom door and then, as sudden as a car bomb, Haylee screeching back at her.

"Oh shit," somebody said, and somebody else laughed.

The screeching increased and the bathroom door flew open, almost bashing me in the face. Haylee shot out of the bathroom, her eyes gleaming and her gauzy lilac dress rippling behind her like a war banner. She pushed through the crowd of students and started running down the hall. Mrs. Daly emerged from the bathroom with her arm around a junior girl named Madison Lambert, who was crying into a bloody wad of paper towels. Mrs. Daly frowned at the gathered crowd and led Madison down the hall toward the principal's office.

"Oh yeah," Sam said, grinning. "Haylee smacked her good."

According to Sam (who sure loved his hallway gossip for such an anti-social dude), Madison Lambert's date had danced with Haylee without asking Madison's permission. Perturbed by this, Madison approached my sister in the bathroom, ugly things were said, and suddenly Haylee smacked Madison so hard her nose started to bleed. Mrs. Daly got called in and there you were: Haylee "Haystack" Druneswald was in deep shit.

The crowd hovering around the bathroom dispersed, but I knew this was only the beginning. These seven or eight students would fan out through the school, repeat the story of the fight to anybody who'd listen, and fifteen minutes from now everybody in Hickson High would know about the fight. A fight over a boy Haylee probably didn't even give a flip about. Everybody would laugh and mock and everything would be about a hundred times worse for little old Haystack.

The only thing that could stem such a gossipy tide would be a bigger story…

A tale of smoke and fire.

"Sam, I need you to watch the bathroom door. Keep everybody away."

"Why?"

"Just do it, man."

I pushed opened the door and went into the girl's bathroom. I gazed at myself in one of the mirrors. I was looking pretty good in my charcoal suit. Like a classy undertaker.

"You shouldn't do this, Mack," I said to Mirror Mack. "This is stupid."

We stared at each other.

Neither of us was backing down.

"You're just trying to justify your dirty little urges. This is not a solution to anything."

Mirror Mack was right, of course. This was the kind of ill-considered stunt that could get me expelled from school, or at least seriously affect my college application if I ever went that route.

Yet the moment was here for the taking. Right now, tonight. Smoke bubbled inside my heart, waiting to escape and rise up.

Was I going to live forever?

No.

Nobody lived forever. Mom sure hadn't.

I grabbed the bathroom's trash can and set it in the center of the room, beneath the fire detector. The can was half full of wadded-up paper towels and tissues and I filled the rest of it with dry paper towels, yanking them from the dispenser in greedy pulls. I pulled a lighter out of my pocket and lit the top strata of towels in several places. While they began to burn I went into a stall and unspooled an entire roll of toilet paper, swathing it around my hand. I fed the smoldering fire with scraps of toilet paper until flames rose steadily from the bin and smoke drifted toward the ceiling.

I left the bathroom and found Sam alone in the hallway, looking worried.

"All right, Sammy. I'd suggest exiting the school right now if you don't want to get your one good suit wet."

"What?"

"Run, Orson, run."

The school's fire alarm erupted and the sprinklers came on in the hallway. Sam swore and started sprinting toward the front doors, moving good for a big man. I went back into the gymnasium, which was now pure chaos as everybody fled, hollering and laughing and shoving each other, the DJ desperately trying to cover his equipment. I found Katrina still sitting in her auditorium seat while sprinkler water rained on her from above, causing her mascara to run and her black dress to cling somehow even more tightly to her body. She grinned as I dropped from the raised gym floor and approached her.

"Did you do this, Mack-Attack?"

I tried my best to look cool, peering off into the distance at the wet chaos by the auditorium's entrance.

"Oh," I said, "you know me."

End Times

When someone is put on an artificial respirator, they are transformed into something even more tenuous than your average human being. They need help. They need help to breathe, to push oxygen through their blood stream, to live to see another day. Besieged by one kind of physical calamity or another, a person on a respirator is no longer able to exist within the cage of their body without the artifice and ingenuity of science. They've become dependant on a machine (which itself is dependant on manipulated electrical current) to do something human beings do every day without conscious thought.

What I didn't expect, the first time I saw my mother on artificial respiration, was how it made her look so different that I thought the critical care nurse had directed me to the wrong room. The woman lying in bed in this room had a rattler's nest of wires and tubes running out of her, with the biggest tube of all crammed into her mouth and secured with white medical tape. The woman in this room was so thin you could almost see her lungs rising through her narrow, concave chest and the white blanket covering it.

This woman, I could clearly see, was fucked.

"Mom?"

I stepped up to the side of the woman's hospital bed and placed my hands on its aluminum railing. The respirator made horrible whooshing sounds in the back corner of the room, really working its ass off. The woman had Mom's shoulder-length brown hair. The woman had a face, behind the tubes and the medical tape, which appeared to be a rough approximation of my mother's face, like a wax museum replica.

The ground shifted beneath my feet. I felt as if I might pitch forward on top of the bed. Right on top of her.

My weight would probably crush her.

End everything.

End times.

We had finally come to the end times.

"I'm sorry," I told her. "I'm sorry I came late."

———

My first urge was to hunker down in that hospital room and refuse to get up again until she woke up. I lasted ten minutes before I had to leave the room, unable to stand the sounds of the beeping monitors and the whooshing respirator and the terrible, unnatural hitch in my mother's chest as she breathed. Was forced, forced to breathe, her body air-raped so she could use it again when she finally woke up.

The problem, my father told me as I rejoined everyone in the waiting room, was that the infection had spread deeper into her lungs while her kidneys were failing. She would remain sedated until her body rallied and she was strong enough to breathe on her own again. I tried to imagine what it would be like to wake with a respirator tube crammed down your esophagus. The panic that would seize you, the immediate urge you'd feel to rip the fucker out. It was like something out of *Alien*, really, but medical professionals had done this to my mother on purpose because they'd felt they had no other choice.

"This is bad, isn't it, Dad?"

"It'll be okay, Mack. She's a fighter."

Haylee, who'd recently turned fourteen, was sitting on the other side of my father, clinging to his arm like a koala cub. Her eyes had gone blank and she was staring into the waiting room floor as if she could see through it to whatever lay below. Grandpa and Grandma Hedley were sitting more naturally on her other side, hands folded on their laps. They had the calm, determined air of older folks who'd spent plenty of time in waiting rooms and understood that the waiting never really ended. I felt a heady urge to stand up and slap both of them—SLAP SLAP—and shout an incoherent stream of obscenities in prelude to running out of the hospital, jumping into my car, and driving until I hit water.

Haylee made a tiny, animal-like sound. My head dropped to my chest. A woman's crackling voice paged some dude named Rick Appleton over the waiting room intercom.

"I should have come sooner. I should have come right away."

Dad put his arm around my shoulder and squeezed me against him. I rested my head against his shoulder.

"Fucking history test."

"It happened so fast, Mack. It's all right."

"But—"

Dad squeezed me again, surprisingly strong for a life-long paper pusher.

"It wasn't very cool there, Mack. Before they put her under."

Haylee made another animal sound and I closed my mouth, pushing away all the useless talk that wanted to flood out of my mouth. Nobody needed to hear me bitch about myself at that moment—we just needed to wait and steel ourselves for whatever terrible thing came next.

Around ten, a doctor came out and told us we could go home for the night. They expected no major changes in her condition. She could be under for several days.

Nobody went back to school or work the next day. Dad, Haylee, and I visited the hospital and spent an hour sitting beside my mother's bed—a horrible, agonizing hour in which the steady whooshing of her respirator resonated throughout my body. The rest of the day we hung around at home, stuffed into our various rooms/cocoons. After Day Two, Haylee and Dad went back to their regular lives. I understood this. They couldn't tolerate sitting still and doing nothing. They knew, we all knew, that each day that passed with Mom unable to breathe on her own made it less likely she'd come back at all. Better to keep busy, busy busy busy, and think about Mom only ninety percent of the time instead of a full hundred percent. Perhaps a watched mother never wakes.

But I wanted the pain that came with worrying about her. I craved it. I thought the pain meant that Mom was still with us, that her life was still in play and its length still undecided. I thought about medical miracles, comeback stories. I thought about praying, really, really thought about it, and finally gave it a try while sitting on her couch, wrapped in her quilt:

God, please let my mom wake up.

God, please don't be an asshole.

I even tried writing. I wrote a story about a woman who's kicked in the head by a horse and lies in a coma for two weeks on the edge of death. Finally, when everything looks bleak as hell, the woman is visited in the night by a cat. The nurses and doctors in the hospital all know about this cat—it's a hospital legend—but nobody's ever managed to catch it. It sort of haunts the hospital, like a ghost, and when it visits the comatose woman in her hospital room, the cat jumps onto her bed, climbs across her body, and lies down on top of her head, right over her bandages. The cat starts purring, louder and louder, and after a few minutes the woman opens her eyes and asks who left the air conditioning on.

———————

On Day Three, Mom's two brothers arrived with their wives and kids. They stayed in a hotel near the hospital in Thorndale and took turns holding vigil beside her bed. They meant well, but their appearance alone was an ominous sign that even I, deluded optimist that I was, could not help but recognize. I called Sam and told him the end was nearing. He surprised me by asking if I'd take him to see her that night, after the other relatives and friends had left the hospital.

Sam's grandmother drove us to the hospital after supper but stayed in the waiting room. Sam and I found Mom alone in her room, surrounded by a small garden of flowers, plants, and get-well cards. She looked smaller than ever, her hands folded across her sunken chest.

"Hey, Mom. I brought Sam."

"Hey," Sam said, stepping up to the bed. "Good to see you, Mrs. Druneswald."

I reached out and held one of Mom's hands. They'd filled with fluid during her forced coma and had grown to three times their normal size, like plastic gloves filled with hot water, or clown hands, and they looked ridiculously huge in comparison to the rest of her. I gave her hand a hard squeeze and imagined I felt a slight squeeze back, a spasm of recognition.

Sam looked around, taking in the machines, the flowers. "She doesn't look so bad, dude."

"You don't think so?"

"No. She looks like she could wake up any time now. They just need to get rid of that monster tube and all that tape. That's some freaky shit."

"I know, right?"

Sam sat down. I took out a folded wad of paper from my back pocket and unfolded it, smoothing out the creases. It was a story I'd written a few years before, a funny one about a hobby chicken farmer who loses his farm to a tornado but manages to save all the baby chicks. Bringing the story and reading it aloud to my mother was Sam's idea. He said it would be better than sitting around in silence like a couple of monks.

I started to read aloud, my eyes darting to my mother's face during each pause, and I read the whole twelve-page story, the room around me gradually retreating as I was drawn into the hobby farmer's trouble. The tornado came, the farmer saved what he could save, and when it was over he had a box of chickadees in his arms, chirping away.

When I looked up from the last line, Sam was watching the heart rate monitor with wide eyes.

"Her heart line changed. It blipped during the funny parts."

"Really?"

"Yeah. Really."

I folded the pages back up and stuffed the story back into my pocket. We watched my mother, wondering.

On Day Five everybody knew the score. Mom's kidneys were failing, her liver was failing, and her heart was weakening. The long siege that had started with a spot of cancer on her lung was winding down and it was up to us to see it mercifully ended. Our entire immediate family, except for the little kids, met with Mom's doctor to discuss taking her off the respirator and letting nature run its course.

We met in a rectangular room that could have been a corporate boardroom except for the overwhelming orange tang of hospital disinfectant and a porcelain washbasin at the far end of the room. We sat in comfortable, high backed leather chairs and stared balefully at the doctor, who'd taken one side of the long table all to himself. He recited the litany of Mom's ills, one by one, and we listened as the list piled up like shovelfuls of dirt all around us.

I felt split by two ideas at once, one rational and the other not:

Mom could no longer go on living.

Mom could not die. Not now, not at thirty-seven.

The two ideas waged war inside my mind, equally powerful, and I understood for the first time what schizophrenia might feel like. I leaned back and gazed at the ceiling, trying to think of nothing. The doctor finished his speech by recommending that we take my mother off artificial respiration and let nature play out while keeping her fully, mercifully sedated. The room was silent for a while. One of my uncles raised his hand, as if he were in school, and asked a question about the sedation. He was stalling, filling the silence. The doctor replied, in excessive detail, and the room went quiet again.

"I want everyone to be on board with this," the doctor said. "I'd like a formal vote, please."

So we went round, one by one, and voted to take Mom off artificial respiration. The only person who voted no was Haylee, who'd started crying.

"She can come back," Haylee said, looking at the rest of us, looking at me. "She can, you guys. She can."

"Honey, it's best this way," Dad said, touching Haylee's arm. "She's been in so much pain."

"No. I don't want to let her go."

My sister wiped her nose with the sleeve of her shirt. Her eyes were bright and feral, like a cornered animal's. She stared us all down like she'd blink us out of existence if she had the power. Like if only we'd believe.

PART TWO

The Emergency Lunch

I felt oddly disconnected as Sam, Katrina, and I watched the commotion from the high school parking lot. My little bathroom fire had definitely got the attention of the authorities—fire trucks, cop cars, and ambulances showed up to Hickson High while everybody stood outside watching in soggy semi-formal wear—but it didn't really provide the thrill I'd been expecting. It was fun for about ten minutes, like a fire drill, but I knew they weren't going to find anything worse than a scorched trash bin.

No. This wasn't exactly *Carrie*. This was amateur hour, really, nothing compared to the fierce wall of fire I'd started at Ox Haggerton's. The firebug had barely gone thumpity when I'd started the trash bin fire and he'd gone back to sleep as soon as the authorities had shown up. He knew pale fire when he saw it.

Something had shifted.

The firebug and I needed more.

When I got home Dad was sitting on the couch, frowning at the TV.

"Mack."

"Father."

"I'm sure you know all about your sister's fight at the dance."

"I heard reports."

"Haylee's having trouble, Mack. Real trouble. She could be suspended."

"Maybe. Maybe not."

My father muted the TV and turned his full attention on me. "You're all wet."

"Yeah. Somebody tried to smoke in the school bathroom or something. The sprinklers went off. It was crazy."

Dad stared at me for a long time. Then he said, "We're going out for an emergency lunch tomorrow, bucko. The whole family."

"An emergency lunch?"

"You heard me."

"I did. It just sounded a little crazy."

We stared at each other some more. I could tell Dad was pretty pissed, so I decided to cut my losses and call it a night.

"Okay. Lunch it is."

I went up to my room and got out of my soggy clothes. The usual post-burn emptiness came over me, with the accompanying self-loathing. If I couldn't control myself, how could I expect my kid sister control herself? Shit. How could I even expect to graduate before I accumulated some serious felony charges?

I went into the bathroom and put my ear to the tiny door above the bathtub, but I couldn't hear anything.

Somehow the silence was worse than crying.

The next morning we took the van into Thorndale. Dad drove, I sat in the passenger seat, and Haylee sat in back, texting on her phone. Chompy lay wedged on the floor between van's front seats with his paws extended, sphinx-like, and drooled profoundly on the van's carpeting.

"Why's the beast along again?"

Dad gave Chompy a scritch on the head. Chompy nipped at his hand and continued drooling.

"He likes riding in the van. He finds it stimulating."

"Yeah, that's what this dog needs. More stimulation."

We came up on an old man driving a rusted pickup truck. Dad changed lanes and accelerated past the oldster, who was a wearing the obligatory camouflage baseball cap and blue denim shirt.

"Who was that?"

"Hell if I know. Your grandpa's the social butterfly, not me."

"You get out," I said. "You sell insurance."

"I mostly supervise these days. Fieldwork is a young man's game. I have an office to run."

Dad turned up the radio and started whistling along

with Fleetwood Mac. He always whistled when he was nervous. He must have been a shitty poker player.

"So," I said, glancing back at Haylee. "What happens at an emergency lunch? Are we all going to start a trust circle and share our feelings? Or is Haylee going to teach us bathroom self-defense?"

Dad scowled. "Don't act like that, Mack."

"Act like what?"

"You know. Flip. Like everything's a joke."

Chompy opened his maw and clamped down on my calf. When I didn't slap him away he gave it a few exploratory chews. I could feel his teeth through the fabric of my jeans, seeking purchase.

"I use humor as a defensive mechanism, Father. Humor is the shell that conceals the tender, meaty pistachio within me."

Dad frowned. "You're full of crap is what you are. I think you like messing with people just to mess with people."

I looked out the window at the passing woods. I knew every roadside billboard, every highway sign. I knew when the highway would dip and rise and dip again as we entered the outskirts of Thorndale. We'd driven this route hundreds of times together, though usually I'd been in the back seat reading a book. The enduring sameness of the drive was both comforting and wildly maddening. I wouldn't have minded seeing the entire route engulfed in flames, in smoke and dragon fire.

How much would such a fire take to start, exactly?

It hadn't rained in a long time.

"You're a good kid, Mack, but you think you're smarter than everybody else and that's not real appealing all the time. Most people don't give a dang how many books you've read. They just want you to be straight with them. You be straight with someone and they'll respect you for it."

I reached down and rapped on Chompy's head. He released my leg and looked up, confused by the interruption.

"Stop chewing on me."

The beast cocked his head.

"Lay down."

The beast barked, waited, and returned to his slow gnawing. I reclined in resignation and looked out my window. Dad whistled off-key and Haylee maintained her silence in the back, rather sphinx-like herself.

———

We went to Serafina's, the best restaurant in Thorndale and our family's favorite. We sat in a vinyl booth by a window. Serafina herself came out to greet us, all smiles and Italian warmth.

"Well, well! What a handsome family we have here."

Dad slid out of the booth, gave the restaurateur a hug, and stood with his arm around her, smiling. Serafina inspected Haylee and me, her smile fading as she focused on my sister. Stout and middle-aged, her dark hair pinned back, Serafina looked capable of heaving a barrel of wine onto her shoulder and hiking up the nearest rocky mountain.

"*Mio dio*. You are so thin, Haylee." Serafina glanced at Dad and clucked her tongue. "You need to feed this girl more, Peter. She's still growing. She needs meat on her bones."

"I eat," Haylee protested. "I eat a lot."

Serafina nodded, still scanning my sister with her Italian lady radar. Dad's face went tight and he shifted on his feet, dropping his arm from Serafina's shoulders and letting it fall limp to his side. Serafina, noticing our collectively weird mood, announced they'd renovated the kitchen and invited Dad back to check it out. Suddenly Haylee and I were sitting in the booth alone, the table's tea light candles burning between us.

I tossed my menu aside and peered back toward the kitchen. "What do you think they're really doing in there?"

"Who cares."

"I bet they're making out. Lots of heavy crotch petting. Lascivious ear licking."

Haylee sighed and crossed her arms. "Fucking Madison Lambert."

"You really smacked her good, huh?"

My sister glanced out the window at the restaurant's parking lot. Chompy, who was not allowed in fine Italian dining establishments, was sitting bolt upright in the van's passenger seat and watching us.

I reached toward one of the table's candles, sweeping my index finger through the flame. Swipe, swipe. It didn't hurt at all. It was nothing. Amateur hour.

"She called me a mommy orphan."

"What?"

"Madison. She called me a sad little mommy orphan, so I hit her."

No victorious smile from the Haystack. Not even a tiny, wry one. Just a deep, Russian-sounding sigh.

"You know what? As soon as I hit her, I thought about Mom. I knew that when I got home later, Mom wouldn't be around to talk about the fight. She wouldn't be on the couch, watching TV with a blanket on her lap and a box of Kleenex by her feet. We wouldn't have tea."

"I loved having tea with Mom," I said, forcing my hands to lie flat on the table. "She was good at having tea."

Haylee blew her nose into her napkin. "She was. She was the fucking best at it."

The candles flickered. I smelled garlic frying in the kitchen. Dad would be back soon, full of more false cheer and fluffy conversation, trying to make this domestic clusterfuck work out.

"Chompy really loves you, you know."

More sniffles and nose-blowing. Haylee's eyes had grown damp and enormous, the flecks of green in each iris glowing in the candlelight.

"He does?"

"Yeah," I said. "I had a talk with him. We agreed, actually. We both think you're pretty awesome and that Madison totally had it coming."

Haylee looked out at the van. Chompy saw us watching

him and whirled around in the passenger seat, pink tongue flying.

Finally, a little smile from Haystack.

Maybe the emergency lunch hadn't been such a dumb idea after all.

Hot Garbage

The following Monday, the fire during the homecoming dance was the talk of Hickson High while Haylee's fight with Madison Lambert was relegated to just another crazy homecoming side story. I walked around the school with my head held high and felt like an honest-to-God do-gooder, a feeling I'll admit I hadn't felt in a long time, and it was if the whole world smiled upon me. I was Good Mack the Good Brother, Even If His Sister Must Never Ever Know About His Secret Arson Career Because She Would Totally Fucking Tell Dad.

This warm and fuzzy feeling lasted until twenty minutes into my afternoon shift at the hardware store, when Ox Haggerton came in while I was facing the shelves. I'd been daydreaming about *Fahrenheit 451* and how weird that would be, to get paid to burn books, and I didn't notice Haggerton until he was right on top of me, scowling and smelling like lighter fluid. He looked even older and more puckered than I remembered, though his eyes were just as red and angry.

"Chainsaws," he said.

"Excuse me?"

"Where are your chainsaws?"

"Oh," I said, wiping my palms on my jeans. "Sure. Let me show you."

I took him to the shelves at the back of the store where we kept the heavy duty stuff. I pointed out the only chainsaw we kept in stock.

"That's all you've got? One goddamn chainsaw?"

"Yes, but we can order any kind you'd like. We don't sell a lot—"

"Fuck ordering," Ox said. "If you don't have it on your shelf I don't want to fucking see it."

He picked up the chainsaw and raised it into the air for inspection. His arms were knotted with tight little old man muscles, stored strength he'd probably gained from a lifetime of adding to the woodpile I'd burned down three weeks before. I waited while he turned the chainsaw over and ran his thumb along the teeth of the cutting chain, frowning like it was a piece of trash he'd found in his backyard.

"This is it? This is all you've got?"

"Yes, sir," I said, fighting a strong urge to walk off and hide in my boss's office. Nobody spoke for a moment and the store's fluorescent lights hummed above us, sounding as demonic as ever.

"I guess it'll do," Ox said, lowering the chainsaw and looking at me. "Hey. I remember you. You're George Hedley's grandson."

"Yes, sir."

"You still working at the Legion?"

"Yes, sir."

"You're a busy little shit, aren't you?"

A vision of Haggerton's woodpile engulfed in glorious flame suddenly filled my mind for one flashing second, as real as if I was standing in front of it again.

"Yes, sir," I said. "I try to keep busy."

———

After Big Greg and I closed the store I came home to find the house empty and dim. Dad and Haylee were in Thorndale at her first therapy session, which was part of her deal with the school to avoid suspension for the homecoming fight. The other part of the deal was for Haylee to personally apologize to Madison Lambert herself, which must have nearly made my sister's head explode.

I let Chompy out of his kennel and took him outside for a pee. Strong winds had turned the woods behind our house into a big, thrashing mosh pit and the effect was a little unnerving.

"What do you think, Chompy? Is Big Foot hiding out there? Watching us, waiting for signs of weakness?"

The beast snatched a fluttering leaf out of the air and devoured it. I led him into the small ravine and up the opposite side to the train tracks. I looked away while he did his business on the rails, staring at the forest's autumn leaves until the colors blurred together. The ground trembled beneath my feet.

"Hey. You feel that?"

The train whistled to announce its approach as I led Chompy back to the ravine's floor. The dog started running back and forth in spastic ecstasy, lunging against his leash and barking like a madman. I dug in my heels and fought an urge to let go and see if the beast would actually charge. Haylee would laugh, I thought. She'd laugh to see her simpleton pooch giving me such a hard time. She'd laugh if she could laugh, if the Dark Ferret of Sadness That Whispered Sorrow Into Her Ear allowed her to recognize the comedy inherent in a skinny, tall guy trying to rein in a worked-up dog.

"Here it comes, dummy," I shouted. "Get ready."

The train's engine emerged thunderously from the woods, its single headlight bright in the fading daylight. Chompy went still, as if understanding his foolishness, and the engine disappeared back into the woods, quick as that. Three minutes of freight cars came rolling behind it, throwing sparks along the rails. Most of the cars carried sealed shipping containers, though a few tank cars and old-school boxcars were thrown into the mix to keep it interesting. It was the boxcars I'd liked best when I was kid. Many was the time I'd imagined stuffing a backpack full of ham sandwiches, sneaking out of the house in the middle of the night, and crossing the little ravine. I'd wait patiently for the next train, sprint alongside it when it finally arrived, and effortlessly leap into the first available boxcar. I'd already be long gone by the time my parents woke up in the morning, three or four hundred miles away. They'd cry their eyes out they'd miss me so much. The whole damn town would cry.

The last cars rolled past. The show was over. Chompy gave one last sharp bark at the woods and looked at me.

"What?"

The dog eyed my car, which was sitting in the driveway. I gave a martyr's sigh and headed up the ravine. Chompy scrambled to catch up, paused to press happily against my side, and then raced ahead to the car. I opened the back door and the beast leapt inside, turning around twice in the back seat before happily settling down, pink tongue lolling. I went around to the driver's side and started the engine, pulling out of the driveway slowly so as not to make a racket. We rumbled through the autumn night and Chompy slid around in the back seat, shifting with the abrupt turns like a panting gym bag. I rolled down my window and we turned onto the highway, just two saucy fuckers headed out for a night on the prowl.

We drove beyond town. I was sick of all the same old houses, the same old streets. Driving faster, on an actual highway, at least provided the illusion of novelty. At seventy miles per hour anything could appear in the Oldsmobile's headlights, at any minute. Bears, vampires, a zombie Charles Bukowski; I'd be happy with anything beyond the usual smorgasbord of Balrog County roadkill.

We drove for a half hour before I noticed Chompy yawning in the rearview mirror.

"What? A free car ride isn't good enough for you?"

The beast stared back at me, his eyes dark and crazed.

"Ah," I said. "I know where you want to go."

I slowed the car down, whipped a U-turn, and headed in the opposite direction. Ten minutes later and the air had turned ripe with the smell of skunky garbage and cardboard, causing Chompy to perk up and stick his head out the window. We drove past the county landfill's entrance and parked discreetly a half-mile down the road, near the rear section of the landfill's fence line. Chompy leapt out of the back seat and started to immediately strain at his leash, somehow gagging and eagerly panting at the same time.

"All right, all right."

The landfill was lit by sodium lamps, but since it was heaped with mounded trash it was impossible to get a clear sightline of anything. Chompy and I might as well have been on the other side of the moon as far as the Fill's night watchman was concerned, and that's the way I liked it. We walked along the rear fence, found the same weak spot known to every no-good teenager in Hickson, and tunneled through to the other side, where the smell of garbage was even stronger.

Chompy bounded from trashy heap to trashy heap, smelling and lifting his leg and smelling some more, so ecstatic I thought his head might explode in a spray of feathers. I shook my head at his exuberance and plugged my nose.

"So you like this locale, sire? Is it to your liking?"

Chompy tore into what looked like a bag of Chinese leftovers, spraying dirty lo mein noodles everywhere. I gave him as much length on the leash as possible, trying to avoid the noodle spray zone. I noticed an interesting heap rising a good twenty feet into the air.

"Holy hell, Chompy. Would you look at that."

I pulled the snorting beast along and examined the lofty heap more closely. It was mostly plastic trash bags bursting with clothes and towels. I pulled out a few T-shirts and sweaters but I couldn't find anything wrong with any of them. It was just a big old heap of discarded clothes, rising to the heavens.

I pulled my lighter out of my pocket and twirled it in my fingers. The firebug woke up and flexed its fiery muscles.

This was it.

This was next level shit right here.

Chompy pulled me backward, straining to return to the more food-based trash. I yanked the leash in reply and the beast writhed on his tether. "You had your turn, beastie. Time for papa to have some fun."

I dug out a hand towel. It was dry and pleasantly coarse. I thumbed the lighter, lit one small corner of the towel, and watched the flame grow and creep across its surface. The firebug started to dance, gyrating to a mad antediluvian beat, and I flung the towel at the tower's base. Chompy barked, not digging the fire, and I allowed him to pull me back to the food trash. While the tower fire slowly smoldered, then spread, Chompy enjoyed more nasty snacks and the night buzzed with energy.

We were all feeding. We were all getting fed.

The Claremont Caves

I n middle school my geology class took a field trip to the Claremont Caves, which are so far north of Hickson they're almost in Leroy County. To go on this fancy pants trip we all needed signed permission slips from our parents and to bring our own bag lunch. None of us had seen the caves before and nobody expected much. We were just glad to get out of school for the day and fuck around on the bus, which was its own sort of casual war zone.

———

The caves were terrifying. We counted two dozen of them. They pocketed the side of a broad limestone hill like open sores and exhaled unnaturally cold winds. It was easy to imagine all kinds of monsters coming out of those dark openings. Creatures of girth and tentacles and teeth.

Our teacher wouldn't let us actually go inside the caves. He said it was too dangerous, but never specified why. He just talked for a while about geology stuff and then we all had lunch beside a murky brown river.

I dreamt about those caves for years.

Grandma's Dream

I woke up early on Tuesday after a long night of sweaty, hot-garbage sleep. I shuffled downstairs, fed Chompy, took him outside for a piddle, and ate some cereal in front of the TV while the beast gnawed happily on my ankle. Around seven-thirty, Dad emerged from his bedroom and shuffled into the kitchen to put on his beloved pot of morning coffee. He'd taken the whole week off from work and was looking even shittier since the homecoming dance, the usual purple sadness rings around his eyes appearing even wider. I decided I'd be best served by finishing my cereal, showering quickly, and heading off to school like a man of purpose.

School, however, was intolerable. I was so tired from my night out at the Fill that I could barely prop myself up at my desk and felt in constant danger of collapsing inward, like a dying star. The teachers yacked, yacked, yacked, but thankfully none of them called on me and I was able to float through the morning unscathed.

By lunch, however, I was dragging something fierce. I drank three sodas and felt nothing, not even the usual sleepy jitters. I reported to our friendly school nurse, told her I wasn't feeling so hot, and by one o'clock I was roaming the streets in the Olds, freed from the surly bounds of education.

Unfortunately, I knew my father would still be home, watching PBS while he waited to take Haylee to her afternoon appointment. I decided to visit the Grotto, where I could sack out in my grandparents' guest room for a couple of hours before I went to work. Besides, I hadn't been to visit my grandparents in a while, having fallen away from my grandsonly duties ever since Grandpa Hedley declared war on the county firebug. I figured it'd be better if I spent as little time with the old man as possible, since he was the sort of fella who might be able to actually smell deceit upon you. He had those burning Vietnam eyes, that hunter's nose.

Grandpa's truck was missing from the driveway but I found Grandma Hedley in the kitchen, pulling a tray of brownies out of the oven. She smiled when she saw me and I gave her a hug.

"How nice. A surprise visit from my favorite grandson."

"Hi Grandma."

"You out of school early today?"

"Yep. I'm not feeling too great."

Grandma Hedley took off her oven mitts and tossed them on the kitchen counter. She looked me over through her trifocals.

"It's been a hard few days, hasn't it?"

"I guess so. It definitely could have been better."

"How's Haylee doing?"

"Better, I think. She started counseling yesterday."

"Oh. I'm glad to hear that."

Grandma took a paring knife out of the knife block and started sawing away at the tray of brownies, carving out squares with grid-like consistency.

"So, where's Gramps? Out yelling at a city council member?"

"I don't know. He's out somewhere. I haven't seen him this worked up in years. He gets up twenty minutes after we go to bed and I can hear him walking around the house, muttering to himself." Grandma Hedley wiped her hands on her apron. "Have a seat, kiddo. Let's try these brownies."

I sat down at the table while Grandma Hedley grabbed plates and silverware. It was no use offering to help at snack time—trying to step in would only get you snapped at with a dish towel. I tried to imagine Katrina like this, apron-clad and happily fussing over a tray of freshly baked brownies, and I literally could not do it. The closest scene I could envision was Katrina setting out Jell-O shots on a table made out of human femurs and illuminated by a burning candelabrum.

Grandma Hedley divvied out the brownies and sat down.

"I had a dream about her, Mack. Last night."

"Mom?"

Grandma Hedley nodded and broke off a corner of her brownie with her fork. She put the piece of brownie in her mouth and chewed thoughtfully.

"I was walking in a forest on a sawdust path. The sawdust looked fresh and clean, as if it had been laid down earlier that day. I followed the path for a long time but it never seemed to get any later, or darker. Finally, I came to a clearing with a cabin in it. The cabin's front door was open and I could see your mother inside."

Grandma Hedley dabbed at the corner of her eyes with a napkin.

"She looked like before, Mack. Healthy. Not so thin."

"Really?"

"Really. She looked wonderful."

I tried to remember Mom looking wonderful. It was hard. I pictured mostly medical tape and plastic tubing.

"She was sitting at a small table, doing something with her hands. I waved and said hello across the clearing, but she couldn't hear me. She kept working at whatever she was working at and didn't look up."

Grandma Hedley ate another piece of her brownie and swallowed. Her eyes had filled with tears again.

"That was it. That was the whole dream."

I sat back in my chair. I hadn't touched my brownie yet.

"Huh. That's crazy."

A rumbling engine pulled up to the house. My grandmother stood up and cleared her plate. The front door slammed and Grandpa Hedley entered the kitchen, swinging his arms and whistling. A true figure of purpose, he'd rolled up the sleeves of his red flannel shirt to reveal his meaty forearms. He was smiling, but when he saw Grandma Hedley drying her eyes at the sink his face darkened and he scowled at me.

"Okay, bucko. What'd you do?"

"Me? Nothing."

Grandpa Hedley put his arm around Grandma Hedley and gave her a squeeze. They reminded me of an old-timey pioneer couple. *We'll tame this hard land, Ma.*

"Your grandmother is obviously crying, Mack. Did you say something smart?"

Grandma Hedley sighed and leaned against my grandfather's shoulder.

"So Grandma's crying and you automatically think it's because of me?"

"I don't know, Mack. You seem pretty squirrely these days, if you ask me."

"Squirrely? I'm squirrely?"

Grandpa Hedley nodded, studying me.

"Squirrely like a squirrel? Like a squirrel with a big fluffy tail, leaping from tree to tree with suicidal abandon? Squirrely like a squirrel putting on weight and burying nuts for winter?"

Grandma Hedley laughed, but my grandfather didn't even crack a smile. He was staring at me like he was trying to see inside my skull and gauge all the cogs and whistles. He stared and stared until I suddenly got paranoid, like mind-reading was something the old Vietnam vet could actually do.

"All right," I said, rising from my chair. "I better get back at it."

"Bye, sweetie," Grandma Hedley said, hugging me. "Thanks for visiting."

I went out and started my car. As I pulled away from

the curb, my grandfather came out of the house and stood on his lawn, watching me drive away. He'd put on his dark aviator glasses and his shoulders were straight and wide, like he could still kick some ass when needed. I gave the old wolf a splashy wave and my best derp face, knowing how much he'd appreciate the comic moment.

Letter to the Editor

Dear Editor,

It's me again, that pesky firebug who's been running circles around the elected officials of Hickson!

First of all, can I say what a great October it's been so far?! Happy October, everybody! What a great month, right? A wondrous time for bonfires and leaf burning and the smell of wood smoke on the air...sorry, there I go, getting all worked up again!

The reason I'm writing again is to clear up a point that's been nagging at me: No, we did not anticipate the scarecrow on Mrs. Klondike's lawn transforming itself into a burning cross. That surprised us as much as it must have shocked poor Mrs. Klondike!

So we're sorry about that. We in no way endorse racist behavior. Actually, we consider ourselves progressive, despite our caveman-like love of the flame, and want everyone to know that none of our actions are in any way politically motivated.

Yours in Christ,
The Firebug

P. S. And that recent fire at the landfill? Yeah, that was me, *[censored]*!

Robinson Park

So, what are you going to show me?" I asked.

"The coolest thing ever, that's what. Or at least it could be."

"It has cool possibility?"

"A shitload of cool possibility."

It was Wednesday. Katrina had texted me to meet at Robinson Park so here we were, rendezvousing like two spies in a noir movie. Before us lay a shadowland of playground equipment that consisted of a sandbox, an elaborate plastic jungle gym, a tetherball pole, a basketball court, and a swing set. Beyond the kiddy park, down a long grassy slope, was a full-sized baseball field, complete with aluminum bleachers, enclosed fence, and outfield scoreboard. Past the field's outfield wall were dense woods.

"My grandpa helped build this park," I said. "He's the town mayor."

"No shit?"

"No shit."

"So you're basically Hickson royalty."

I stretched out my arm and put it around Katrina's shoulders. "Sure am, miss."

She gave me a soft elbow to the ribs and shrugged off my arm. "C'mon."

We walked into the park. We sat on the swings and started pumping our legs slowly, warming up. The swing's chains felt cold and lumpy in my fists.

"So you wanted to show me the playground in Robinson Park?"

"Close." Katrina added some leg to her swing, pointing out her toes. "It's nice to be out of the house. My roommates are driving me crazy."

"Yeah?"

"They're always trying to be so fucking cool. So hipster. One's a film major, one's a theater major, and one's a visual art major."

"Jesus."

"I know. Every house meeting is like a reality TV episode. I can't even keep track of who's pissed at who anymore and we've only lived together for, like, two months. It's ridiculous."

I pumped my legs faster, gathering velocity. The swinging made me feel queasy but I still liked the lift. The sense that I could, at any moment, leap off and propel myself into space. Soon we both reached the zenith of the swings' height, really rocking it, and Katrina counted down from three as the swing set's metal frame creaked loudly, as if it might collapse at any moment.

At one, we both let go and flew forward. We hovered

above the earth, weightless, and then we landed, thudding feet-first into the sand.

Katrina whooped and pumped her fist in the air. "Hell yeah. Did you feel that lift?"

"I did."

"That lift is what my roommates don't get. They wouldn't have even got on those swings unless they were being ironic about it. Like they were cheesy characters in a rom-com or something."

"You're saying they wouldn't be able to enjoy the swings as swings, per se. They would dismiss the inherent joy of simply flinging yourself across a sandpit."

Katrina punched me in the shoulder. "Right! They'd be embarrassed by actually liking it."

"They've lost touch with their inner child."

"Exactly." Katrina sighed and took my hand. "That's what I like about you, Mack. You're past all that fronting bullshit. You're so honest you're like a simpleton."

"Thanks."

"I mean it," Katrina said, squeezing my hand. "You like fire, so you go out there and light some fires. You don't give a fuck what society says about that, or how much shit you could get into if you got caught. You listen to your heart."

"Yes, but my heart may be insane."

"Who gives a shit? You're not really hurting anyone, are you?"

I scratched my head with my free hand and tried to follow this reasoning. I'd never imagined lighting shit on fire to be admirable in any way—more like a furtive pleasure on par with masturbating in a movie theater.

Katrina led the way down the grassy slope to the baseball field. When we were behind the backstop, she let go of my hand and pressed up against the chain-link fencing. The field had a single streetlamp of its own.

"Check it out."

I came up beside her and peered through the fence. A dark rectangular shape lay out in center field.

"What the hell is that?"

"That's the base of it. They're building a haunted castle for Halloween."

"The city is?"

"Yep," Katrina said, nodding and turning to me. "And guess what? They're making it out of straw bales. Straw bales piled two stories high."

I licked my lips, squinting at the murky shape in center field. I reached out and grabbed a handful of chain-link. It felt real.

"Something like that would light up the whole night," Katrina said. "One little match."

I closed my eyes, imagining the profound glory of such a blaze.

"It's a setup," I said. "My grandpa's trying to catch the county firebug. I bet this whole thing was his idea."

"So? This is what you do, Mack. You're like me: a primal soul hell-bent on enjoying existence at its very source.

We're artists. I build goth bird houses, you write stories and light shit on fire."

I opened my eyes and surveyed the field.

She had me there.

The Trouble with Drinking

Haylee seemed to do all right with her first week of therapy and nobody gave her much shit at school, as far as I could tell. Dad, on the other hand, appeared thrown by the homecoming incident in a way that seemed vastly out of proportion to the event itself. I don't know if it was because of what he was discussing with Haylee's therapist, or if the fight had dredged up some sad stuff about Mom, but the man was seriously off-kilter. He didn't go to work, he didn't call Bonnie. He ate a lot of Captain Crunch and pizza, which was no longer a special Friday treat but our nightly meal, and he watched countless hours of PBS programming, keeping the volume so low that it felt as if the Devil were whispering sweet evils in your ear. This was not the Pete Druneswald I'd known my entire life: a steady, hardworking man who'd seen his beloved wife through five years of complicated ailments without losing hope.

By Thursday night I couldn't stand it anymore. "Dad," I said, grabbing the remote and turning off the TV. "We're going out."

"Mack, I don't feel—"

"I don't give a goddamn monkey how you feel. We're going out, and we're going to have fun."

"What about your sister? We can't just leave her home alone."

"She left twenty minutes ago. She's sleeping over at Staci's house."

"What? On a school night?"

"You said she could. Like, at dinner."

"Oh. I did?"

"Jesus, man. Shave that crappy beard and let's go."

"Are you sure—"

"Rise, O Ancient One! Rise!"

———

Dad spruced himself up, I put Chompy in his kennel, and we hit the highway in the van. I drove and Dad sat in the passenger seat, peering out his window. I turned left off Main Street and onto the four-lane highway, headed south. The sun had already set and creatures of the night were emerging.

Dad glanced at me. "We're not going to Thorndale?"

"No sir. That town's got too many haunts in it."

"So ... Dylan?"

"That's right, buddy."

Dad grunted and turned back to his window. We turned onto a winding two-lane that led to Dylan. Trees crept toward the road and remained thick all the way into town, another fifteen miles of classic rock radio, slow moving pickup trucks, and the occasional bat fluttering across the road.

The road dipped and we descended into a wooded valley. Dylan, home to twelve thousand and change, lay spread out on the valley floor, brightly lit amid the dense, woodsy darkness. Night or day, Dylan was a surprisingly pretty and well-organized burg, especially by Balrog County standards. A sawmill was set on its northern edge, right off the highway, so the lumber trucks servicing the mill didn't need to drive through town. South of the mill sat two gas stations and three fast food joints, followed by a handful of bars and restaurants, with a few stores and a grocery outlet bringing up the rear. Residential homes, a K-12 school, and a town park covered the rest of the valley floor. The town's nicest homes, and some of the oldest, sat perched along the wooded valley ridge so their owners could look down on the commoners below. Mom had often joked that she'd move us to the Dylan hillside someday so she could send us off in the morning dressed like lumberjack royalty.

"Which glorious tavern shall it be, Father?"

"I don't care, Mack. You pick."

"Ah, come on. Don't be like that."

"All right. How about the Log Jam?"

"An excellent choice, sir."

We pulled into the Log Jam's parking lot, which was crowded for a Thursday night, and parked between two mud-spattered pickup trucks. Smokers stood huddled in clumps of twos and threes outside the bar's entrance. I stood tall and fell into step beside my father, who was walking like a condemned man across the parking lot, eyes fixed on the ground. I could feel the smokers watching us as we approached, scanning us for familiar features and finding us lacking, outsiders on their Dylan turf, men not to be trusted. A sad middle-aged man and his goofy string-bean son.

The smokers parted for us, nodding politely enough as we passed. I nodded back, unable to decide if I should smile or if they'd see that as a sign of weakness. Dad opened the bar's front door and I followed him inside.

The Log Jam was warm, loud, and filled with a surprisingly large amount of youngish, attractive-ish ladies.

"Fuck yeah," I said, slapping Dad on the back. "Watch out, Dylan. The motherfucking Druneswalds are in town."

"Please, Mack," Dad said. "We're in public."

The best thing about Dylan was the bars in town never carded you, at least not if you were as tall as I was and accompanied by an adult. Dad and I sat at the bar like true drinking men. Like sailors on shore leave, or cassocks at happy hour. Looking around, it was clear that the Log Jam's rugged décor made the Hickson Legion look like Pussyville, USA. The walls were covered by a delightful collection of circular saw blades, some as big as hay bales, and framed black-and-white photos of old-timey loggers doing their thing: bare-chested muscle men with curling mustaches chopping down trees, standing on top of fallen trees, and hauling trees with teams of horses. Life in Dylan had apparently involved an epic multigenerational war against the area forests.

"You know, I think Katrina would love this place."

Dad turned on his stool. "Who's Katrina?"

"Ah ... she's this girl I've been seeing."

"Dating?"

I scratched my head. "Not exactly. I just see her from time to time, around town. When that happens, we hang out. Usually."

"Well, wear a condom."

"Dad—"

"Your mother had the sex talk with you, right? She said she did."

I laughed and took a sip of my whiskey neat. Dad was nursing one sad little bottle of lite beer.

"Yeah, Dad. We got that all settled, like, ten years ago."

"Good. I've got my hands full enough with your sister right now without adding some unexpected teen pregnancy to the mix."

"You got it, Pops. I'll lay off the baby-making."

A lady shrieked loudly at the back of the bar, having a good time. The room had grown louder in the short time we'd been sitting at the bar. It was only seven o'clock, but I figured Dylan was the sort of burg where the weekday carousing peaked by ten. You didn't want to show up to work at a sawmill too hung over, not if you valued your fingers and limbs.

The waitress swooped by with two beers and two shots of whiskey, though we hadn't ordered another round yet. "Thanks," I said, cutting Dad off before he could protest the extra drinks. I nudged a whiskey into his hand and held up my own.

"I'd like to propose a toast."

Dad eyed the whiskey.

"C'mon, man. Don't leave me hanging."

Dad picked up the shot and held it tentatively in the air.

"To Haylee standing up for herself," I said.

Dad frowned. "No, Mack. To Haylee finding peace."

We clinked glasses. Dad threw his whiskey back like an old pro and I choked on mine in a rather uncool fashion.

"That's good," I said, sputtering. "That must be the good stuff."

"That was shit," Dad said. "Well whiskey."

"Really? I liked it."

Dad sipped his second beer and looked up at the ceiling. "Well, Mack. If your mother only saw us now."

I looked around the room, as if my mother could be hiding behind one of the burly locals. Stowed away in their shaggy beards, perhaps, made small and pocket-sized by death.

"This isn't so bad, is it?"

"I don't know, kid. You tell me."

"We're all still together. She'd like that. And Haylee's going to be fine. We'll get her all therapied up and she'll be as good as new. And we've got a dog now, too. Good ol' Chompy."

"I thought you hated that dog."

I drummed on the bar. "Just sort of. He can fucking hunt some pheasants, anyway. You should have seen that beast out with us, running hither and yon. Even Grandpa Hedley was impressed."

Dad took another sip of his beer. He'd begun to hunch over the bar, like a pill bug curling inward.

"The old codger blames me, you know."

"For what?"

"For her dying."

"What?"

"I was supposed to take care of her. His baby girl."

"But it was cancer—"

"Doesn't matter. It's not a rational thing, Mack. I married his daughter and she died on my watch. That's all he cares about."

I drank my beer and tried to summon a counter argument.

"We had an unspoken contract," Dad said, taking a long sip of his beer. "A gentleman's agreement."

———————

The evening softened as we settled into some serious drinking. Time passed in waves, speeding up and slowing down for no apparent reason. Locals joined us at the bar, their outsider-related shyness melting with each passing round. I found myself saying, "You know, I think Hickson is actually a town on the rise," and ridiculous shit like that while the Dylanites told us stories about union strikes, horrific chainsaw accidents, and rogue logs breaking free and crushing men from the waist down—it was as if we'd stumbled into an old Bruce Springsteen song.

Then it was two a.m. and I was driving the van down a foggy highway. Dad was in the passenger seat, conked out. "We're going home," I announced to no one in particular. The highway had two lanes and was lined with trees. It would ... connect us to the four-lane, which would ... lead us back to Hickson.

Dad started to snore.

A Rush song came on the radio and I sang along, feeling fine.

A blur shot onto the highway, twenty yards distant. I screamed like a girl and slammed on the brakes, throwing the minivan into a hard spin. Something thumped off the van, I screamed some more, and the van came to a rocking stop.

Dad stared out the windshield in dazed shock. I turned down the radio.

"You okay?"

Dad grunted and fumbled with his seat belt, his arms T-Rex clumsy.

"Deer," I said. "Came out of nowhere."

More fumbling and Dad finally got himself unbuckled. He opened his passenger door and flung himself out, landing hard on the road.

"Jesus," I said, unbuckling myself. My entire body was vibrating. I opened my door and stumbled out of the van, using the door to steady myself. The van itself didn't look so bad—some crumpling along the hood. A big dent.

"Dad?"

My father was standing on the edge of the highway ditch, looking down. He was lit up by the van's headlights like an actor on stage. I commanded my legs not to buckle and staggered to his side. A brown, furred creature lay at the bottom of the ditch, partially obscured beneath a screen of fog. It looked unbloodied, yet was twisted at an unnatural angle.

"Shit, Mack," Dad said. "It was a doe."

I stumbled into the foggy ditch and knelt beside the deer. It had four white spots on its side and two more on its flank. I touched its side. It wasn't breathing, but it was still warm.

I heard my father's footsteps crunching up on the road.

"All right," he shouted. "I'm driving."

The Mayor's Corner

Dear Residents of Hickson,

Fall is in full swing and with the changing of the seasons our streets and gutters are filled with dead leaves and twigs. Please make sure you get that lawn raked before the snow falls. I happened to drive around last week on yard waste collection day and noticed many lawns still covered with fallen leaves. I have to say, I was a bit disappointed. Whatever happened to the get-up-and-go that made this country great?

For those of you still mowing your lawn, please remember to *NOT* blow grass into the city streets. Our hard-working municipal workers already have their hands full with seasonal street cleaning without dead grass adding to the mess.

Finally, Halloween is approaching fast and I know the kiddies are busy working on their Halloween costumes. To celebrate the season, the Hickson City Council has decided to hold a special celebration in Robinson Park. The Hickson American Legion is sponsoring a haunted house and boy, it's going to be a doozy, so make sure you bring the kids by for frights and fun.

The haunted house opens on Friday and runs through Sunday from 5-10 p.m. each night. We are still looking for "ghoulish" volunteers, so please contact city hall if you're interested in helping out.

Have a safe and happy Halloween, everyone. If you see vandalism of any shape or form, please call the police immediately. Remember: where there's smoke, there could be an arrest.

Sincerely,
Mayor George Hedley

The Graveyard Party

Every year Sam threw a party for his parents on the anniversary of their passing.

Usually the party consisted of only Sam and I, setting off fireworks and guzzling a filched bottle of his grandmother's apple schnapps, but this year Sam invited Haylee and Katrina to join us and, surprisingly, both females accepted the invitation. On Friday I called in sick to both the hardware store and the Legion and picked everybody up in the Olds, driving slow while recalling the deer I'd hit the night before. I drove us to the peninsula graveyard that jutted out onto Baker Lake and we parked near the entrance, the four of us piling out of the car like it was a day at the zoo.

It was already dusk and night was coming on fast. Haylee and Katrina started on ahead while I got the bag of fireworks out of the trunk and Sam fucked around with something in his backpack. As I shut the trunk, Sam appeared at my elbow holding a liquor bottle.

"Whoa, sailor. That's not schnapps."

"Somebody gave my grandma vodka last Christmas. I don't think she even remembers getting it anymore."

"I should have brought some mix."

Sam grinned and pulled a second bottle from his backpack. "I hope you like generic citrus soda. I've even got ice and plastic cups."

"Well shit. You're pulling out all the stops this year, my friend."

The ladies had walked ahead of us and looked pretty intensely involved in conversation. Sam and I made a beeline across the peninsula for his parents' graves, which were set beside each other in the graveyard's newish front section. The graveyard's lawn was short and brown from the prolonged drought and a ring of dead leaves had piled around each gravestone like a leafy halo. Sam unpacked the cups and drinking materials as Haylee and Katrina slowly made their way over to us. Katrina said something, waving her hand in the air like she was shooing away a bee, and Haylee actually laughed.

Sam poured ice into four plastic cups. "This is the life," I said. "Out drinking in nature."

"A fancy man's picnic," Sam said. "We're like a Monet painting."

"We should be wearing white."

"Yes. White everything. And I wouldn't mind a monocle right now."

"And a long-stemmed pipe carved from the finest briar. I would smoke it expertly and rings of smoke would rise around me in the classiest fashion."

"Shit. That would be classy."

The ladies joined us and sat down in the grass. We were all wearing jeans and warm jackets and had prepared for the cool October evening. A fisherman in a little boat buzzed around on Baker Lake, heading home as the sky darkened.

"Welcome everyone," Sam said, raising the bottle of vodka. "Welcome to the seventh annual Jim and Penny Chervenik Memorial Party."

Sam bowed and we clapped politely. The breeze picked up and you could smell Baker Lake in all its algaeic glory.

"As is tradition," Sam said, "we shall begin with a pour out for my homies."

Sam broke the seal on the vodka, unscrewed the cap, and gave the grass above each of his parent's graves a three second pour. We all clapped again.

"They were good people," Sam said, growing damp-eyed as he stared at the ground. "They weren't rich, good looking, or good at sports, but they'd help a dude out. My dad liked to whittle gnomes and trolls and grilled steak and hamburgers every night, even in the winter. My mom liked reality television and enormous jigsaw puzzles."

Sam took a pull from the bottle and wiped his mouth. I glanced at Haylee and Katrina and noted they were both watching Sam with a hundred percent of their attention, their feet tucked beneath them cross-legged style.

"My parents didn't deserve to die, but they died any-way. They died because an overworked trucker fell asleep and swerved into their lane and smashed them to Kingdom

Come. And you know what? That's life, my friends. That's life. Shit happens."

Sam wiped his eyes and handed me the bottle. He puffed out his cheeks and exhaled loudly.

"Okay, Mack. Why don't you prepare the celebratory libations for our guests."

"Yes sir."

I poured three vodka/lemon-lime cocktails, adhering to a ratio of two-thirds mix to one-third vodka, and made a fourth with just soda in it, which I handed to my sister.

"Hey. I want vodka."

"Sorry, Haystack. You're a minor."

"We're all minors."

"Yes, but you are even more minor. Also, Dad would cut off my head if he found out I gave you hard booze."

Haylee scowled, her jaw setting as she stared into her cup. I could feel a smacking rage building up behind her eyes.

"Here," Katrina said, holding out her own cup. "You can share with me."

Haylee raised her head and took the cup. She stared me down as she took a gulp, handed the cup back to Katrina, and swished the cocktail around inside her mouth. Then her green-flecked eyes widened, locking on to a new thought, and she sprayed the drink into the air, coughing and sputtering as she grabbed her throat.

"It burns!"

The rest of us laughed as she writhed on the ground,

making a real scene of it. We drank our libations and watched the bats come out.

It was already the best party I'd ever been to.

―――――――

We started setting off fireworks when it was dark enough and we all had a solid buzz going. We didn't have anything too big or bright—just bottle rockets and sparklers. Hardly anything for the cops or even the firebug to get excited about.

But still.

The firebug was paying attention.

"We should visit Mom while we're here," Haylee said to me, waving a lit sparkler in the air, her elfin face serious in the dark. "She's right up front."

"I need more to drink first," I said. "We all do."

"Your mom was awesome," Sam said, waving his own sparkler in the air. "You remember that bat? The one we caught?"

Katrina pulled out her pack of cigarettes and lit one, studying Sam from across her spot in the circle. "You guys caught a bat?"

"Yeah," Sam said, still studying his sparkler. "Five or six years ago Mack and I were watching a late-night movie in his living room when this bat came out of nowhere and started flapping around. It was kind of freaky because Mack's dad was out of town and everybody else but us was sleeping, right? So we grabbed a broom and a tennis racket and we chased the bat around for, like, ten minutes. Finally Mack swatted it out the side door and we were all hell yeah, bat, this is our turf!"

Sam laughed.

"Then Mack's mom got up and we had cookies and hot chocolate to celebrate. Even though it was so late at night."

I pictured the three of us at the kitchen table, Sam and I happily dunking cookies in the hot chocolate while Mom drank her herbal tea, smiling a happy Mom smile. She never minded getting up in the middle of the night. She liked the company.

"She called them Victory Cookies," I said.

"Right," Sam said. "Victory Cookies. Like she was so proud of us just for catching a stupid bat."

The sparklers had fizzled out, leaving us in the dark. You could see the end of Katrina's cigarette glowing red.

"Maybe she's still around," Haylee said, her voice sounding soft and small. "Maybe Mom's watching us right now."

"Like a ghost?" Sam said.

"I don't know. Like something."

I took another drink as my buzz threatened to leave me. Beyond the graveyard you could see the surface of Baker Lake shimmering faintly with starlight, the darkness of its shoreline broken by the occasional house light. A train whistle sounded a mile away, most likely passing through our own backyard.

"I believe in spirits," Katrina said. "When I had a bad fever once, I saw my grandmother sitting beside my bed.

She'd been dead for two years but she was there, knitting a blanket for me. She asked me how I was feeling and I turned over and went back to sleep."

"Really?" Haylee said.

"Really. When I woke up, she was gone but my fever had broken. My mom said I'd been up to one hundred and three degrees. She smiled when I told her about Grandma, but I knew Grandma had been there. I could still smell her perfume."

The train whistled again, sounding closer.

"That's cool," Sam said. "I wish my parents would come visit me."

I took out my lighter and reached around in the grass until I found a pack of sparklers. I lit one, used it to light two more, and stuck all three sparklers into the ground in the center of our circle, where they burned fresh and bright for a few fleeting moments, showing how serious everyone had gotten as they turned inward to their own thoughts. Around us, the dark night waited patiently to take over again.

Beechnut

Six miles southeast of Hickson is a micro-town called Beechnut (pop. 89) which is basically a gas station, two blocks of houses, and a little graveyard.

I once sat next to a kid from Beechnut in civics class. When I asked him what he did out there, he said he liked to fool around with a chubby neighbor girl who was so bored she'd let him do just about anything. The first time they fooled around, she pulled her pants down all the way to her ankles while they were out ditch-walking and let him finger her about a hundred feet from her mother's front door. He said she bled like crazy because she hadn't popped her cherry yet.

Whenever I imagine this scene, I can't help adding the sound of a fierce prairie wind, howling and lonely and ever present.

Recon

On Saturday night I called in sick again to my gig at the Legion, which did not seem to surprise nor bother my boss Butch very much. After a nourishing dinner of pizza and cola I took a shower, threw on my least smelly clothes, and picked Katrina up at seven sharp.

Katrina smoked as I drove, looking out at the dark town like an empress surveying one of her lesser territories.

"Does this count as a date?"

Katrina blew smoke through her nostrils and considered the smoke. "Why, Mack? Are you trying to fence me in?"

"I don't know," I said, turning left toward the park. "I wouldn't mind knowing where we stand."

Katrina smiled and knocked cigarette ash through the crack in her window. "We're having a good time. I guess that's where we stand."

The Olds bounced as it struck a pothole. It occurred to me that Katrina was not the type of girl who would enjoy fucking a clingy, whiny, high school bitch boy and that it would be best to keep my cards close to my chest for the time being. Not that I really had any cards to play, anyhow. One night of bourbon-inspired passion was already far more than I'd expected. As far as I or any other non-wealthy, average-looking small town Joe was concerned, I had already run the table in this particular hottie encounter and anything else that came my way now would be a bonus, like finding a quarter on the street after winning the state lottery.

We ran into traffic and had to park several blocks away from Robinson Park. It was cold out and we were bundled in fall coats and stocking caps. The street that led to the park was filled with parents and their kiddies, the younger grubs latched on to their parents' hands while the older ones ran ahead, free-range style. The air was filled with much shouting and laughing and unheeded motherly admonishments. It reminded me of the county fair in Dylan.

Katrina hooked her arm through mine. "Opening night's big around here, huh?"

"Well, Hickson's not known for a plethora of cultural events."

"Those kids are cute."

The kids were cute, from what I could make out in the light of the streetlamps. Many wore costumes though Halloween wasn't until the next day. I saw a shorty Batman scoop a pile of leaves from the gutter and drop them on a shorty pink princess. As the shorty princess twirled and screeched, shorty Batman cackled and sprinted into the night, one more good guy gone bad.

We turned off the street and entered the park's parking lot, which was crammed with cars and trucks and folks chatting in the slim spaces in-between. Kids darted around and played tag. Katrina slapped her sides, a happy little jumping jack.

"Hell yes. Are they actually tailgating this shit?"

"Looks like it."

The playground was packed with kids. The swings, the jungle gym, the sandbox, the merry-go-round—there was action everywhere. A line of parents and kids ran from the edge of the playground all the way down to the castle on the baseball diamond. Katrina and I skirted the playground, eyeing the swarm of kids warily, and got in the back of the line.

The haunted castle was impressive. It was no longer a glorified hayride; they'd built an actual wooden frame for the structure, two full levels with two front towers. Gaps had been left in the walls to serve as windows and you could see strobe lights flickering inside. Halved straw bales formed a crenellated battlement that ran from tower to tower, which were also crenellated. People stood on top of the towers and waved down to the line below like royalty.

"Whoa. Your gramps has been busy."

I rubbed my hands together and blew hot air into them. "Grandpa Hedley doesn't do anything half-assed. You should see their backyard. It's like Italy exploded."

The line moved as a group of giggly teens exited the castle. We passed through a gate in the baseball diamond's fence and walked onto the infield. You could hear screams coming from the castle, both recorded and real.

"You think your grandpa really did all this just to catch you?"

"It's likely."

"Huh. My grandpa reads Westerns all day and barely leaves his recliner. I guess you should be happy yours is staying involved."

I noticed a black flag protruding from the castle's battlement, snapping crisply in the cold wind. At first I assumed it was a pirate's flag, or something equally devilish, but as I looked closer I saw it was an old POW/MIA flag.

I pointed the flag out to Katrina. "Look how serious he is. This is his War of the Worlds. His Siege of Gondor."

"What?"

"Fuck me silly. You know what? I think he got that flag from the Legion."

The mom ahead of us in line turned around and glared at me. She had big hairspray-lady hair.

"There are children here," she hissed. "Watch your mouth."

I held up my palms. "This is a haunted castle. You don't think the Devil lets a salty word fly now and again?"

"The eternally danged," Katrina said. "Little heckians."

The lady made an angry horsey sound and turned back around, clutching her two chunky fledglings to her waist.

"Tough crowd," I said. Katrina laughed and slid her hand into the back of my jeans, cupping my ass. When the ticket lady reached us, I paid for two and the line surged forward again. Lo, soon we had passed beneath that Unsettling Black Flag and entered those Mighty Straw Walls, where we were subjected to Numerous Ye Olde Terrors that would drive Many a Mortal to the Brink.

It was the kind of corny shit Mom would have loved.

After we'd recovered from our Mortal Terror, we headed back to Katrina's house and found her roommates throwing a loud party. Her roommates were as hipster and dramatic as advertised—I counted five fussy arguments in the first half-hour—but I was in the mood for drinking and threw myself into the festivities with the best of them.

Around midnight I found myself standing outside the house with a bunch of dudes I didn't know. More than half-drunk, I suggested we get a bonfire going. This idea was greeted with a bunch of fuck yeahs but the only firewood we could find was a starter log in the house's fireplace. The dudes were disheartened but I remembered the basement, crammed full of flammable shit, and led us downstairs while everyone else was busy arguing about the various cinematic adaptations of *Les Misérables*. I directed the dudes toward whatever looked like it would burn best, making certain they left Katrina's birdhouses alone, and we started hauling the more flammable junk upstairs, careful to stay on the party's perimeter. We brought out three loads before Katrina and her roommates caught on to our game, but by then we'd created a tantalizing pile of burnables in the backyard. Everybody pitched in for one more load and we hauled more basement junk out *en mass* and piled it high.

"Jesus, Mack," Katrina said, tossing a cardboard box full of magazine onto the pile. "My birdhouses aren't in there, are they?"

"Nope. I kept the drunkards away from your workshop."

The partygoers around us started chanting fire, fire, fire, which rattled the firebug's cage and rebooted my highly suggestible brain. The college dudes looked at me, their self-appointed leader, and I knew the time had come. I used a lighter, a few twists of newspaper, and the starter log to kindle the junk heap's center. The moldy boxes and lacquered furniture took a while to catch, but I had the dudes scoop up dry leaves and twigs from the yard and toss them into crucial spots, warning them not to choke the fire. Eventually, with the help of the wind, the flames found an ugly wicker chair that went up like a torch and the heap erupted.

Sometime around three a.m. I noticed Katrina standing outside the group, talking on her phone. I ambled over to her, feeling drunk and unusually cool after the fire's success.

" … I don't care, Mom. No. I don't care."

I took a pull from the beer in my hand. Katrina's brow was furrowed and her eyes gleamed with firelight.

"Who the fuck knows? He was at a bar, right? Maybe

he got in a car accident. Maybe he's dead on the side of the road."

"Maybe he hit a deer," I drunkenly interjected, wondering who we were even talking about. "I hit a deer recently and it was quite traumatic."

"You always do this. You always want sympathy when he pulls shit but then you take him back. Every fucking time you do this."

Katrina rolled her eyes as a squall of static sound erupted from her phone.

"I'm hanging up now, Mom. Yes, I am. Sorry. Give Bill my worst."

Another squall of static noise. Katrina powered off her phone and slipped it into the front pocket of her jeans.

"Jesus Christ. My mom's, like, the drama queen of the century. She and Bill fucking deserve each other."

I nodded agreeably, regretting having left the bonfire's comforting warmth and my new carefree drinking buddies. Katrina glowered and stared off into the night, arms crossed.

"Beer?" I said, offering her the half-full can in my hand.

Katrina looked at me as if noticing me for the first time and accepted the beer. She downed it in one gulp and chucked the can into the dark.

"Let's go in, Mack."

"What about—"

"Come on."

Katrina's hand gripped my own, pulling me toward her house. She brought me inside, up the stairs, and into her bedroom. She took my clothes off so quickly I almost fell over and suddenly she was naked, too. We smelled like wood smoke. Katrina tasted like salt and lime. From time to time I raised my head, looking out the window to check on my crackling work below.

You Are My Sunshine

Our family remained in the meeting room while they removed Mom's respirator tube, crumpled in our chairs.

We'd voted to let her go.

It was time to let her go.

We did not want to let her go.

———

A nurse came to get us. She asked who wanted to be with her at the end and I rose from my seat without thinking. Haylee stood up too, though her skinny legs wobbled, threatening to spill her. We followed the nurse out the door, and when I looked back I was surprised to see nobody else trailing us. Not Mom's brothers, not Grandpa and Grandma Hedley. They stared at the floor, as limp as if someone had cut their strings. They'd already said goodbye, I realized. Even Dad, good old Dad, sat hunched over in his chair as if he'd been socked in the stomach. His blurry red eyes met mine and dropped back to the floor.

Haylee took my hand and pulled me forward. We followed the nurse down a long hallway I didn't exactly recognize and entered another I knew all too well. We were kid explorers, Hansel and Gretel in a hospital. We entered a room and there was Mom, lying on a hospital bed. As advertised, her breathing tube had been removed and the respirator was finally silent. Her eyes were still closed—they'd pumped up the sedatives and morphine to just this side of fatal. Her skin had turned yellow, her hands were as water-bloated as ever, and she was gasping.

Great, hitching gasps. An animal reduced to its purest form. Her entire emaciated frame writhed with each inhalation, her head convulsing slightly to the left. So much oxygen in the room and she couldn't use any of it.

I breathed deeper, as if I could breathe for her, and cheered her on with every molecule in my useless body. Haylee circled the bed and took her right hand. I stepped up and took the left. It felt so warm and heavy.

"We're here, Mom," Haylee said. "We love you."

It could take several minutes, the doctor had warned us. The body fighting on after the war had been decided.

The hitching got worse.

More desperate.

I told my mom I loved her. That we all loved her so much. The nurse came up and put her arm around Haylee, who'd started to cry and smile at the same time. I was not crying. I was too busy trying to breathe and channel the breathing. I felt a coldness fall upon my shoulders and knew Death had entered that sterile room.

Not movie death, not book death.

Death.

"Does your mother have a favorite song?" the nurse asked. "We could sing it to her."

Haylee sniffled and nodded. She wasn't fourteen anymore—she was four. "'You Are My Sunshine.'"

I frowned, unable to understand why Haylee had picked that song. Mom had sung that to us when we were little but her favorite stuff had been '60s classic rock, like Joplin and Hendrix.

Then Haylee and the nurse started singing the goddamn song and it was too late to argue. I started singing too, though I was filled with a new and powerful rage, a rage stronger than anything I'd ever felt in my entire life. Who was this old lady nurse, who was she to intrude on our last moments with Mom? Why did Haylee have to pick this fucking song? Why couldn't Mom FUCKING BREATHE—

I noticed movement in the corner of my eye.

Dad had poked his head into the room. Just his head, as if the hospital bed inside were radioactive. His eyes were big and full of so much love I felt my rage blown apart, a pile of leaves scattered by a gale force wind. Dad stepped inside the room, came up to Mom's bed, and wrapped his hands around one of her feet. He didn't say anything. He just stood there, holding her foot and watching, while the rest of us sang like a bunch of cheesy singing assholes. The spasmodic hitching breaths worsened, then lessened, then lessened in an alarming way. We ran out of song and fell silent. Mom's body sank into the bed, remained still for a good thirty seconds, and gave one last gasp before she was thoroughly gone.

The Windmill

There's a southeastern patch of Balrog County where even trees don't feel like growing. It's mostly grassland lumped with rocks and notable only for an enormous windmill a hippie built in the early 1970s. He'd been smoking peyote and drinking bathtub gin when Don Quixote spoke to him in a thunderous voice, demanding that he build a working windmill fit for giants.

The hippie built the windmill by himself in one summer, sleeping only three hours a night. He charges people five bucks to visit and take the windmill tour. Besides windmill-related maintenance, he hasn't worked a day since.

The Castle

Halloween arrived like a flaming-scream skull and I found it mighty difficult to concentrate on anything. Time passed slowly and the firebug paced restlessly inside my heart. An impatient creature at best, it knew the time of our greatest triumph was at hand and saw no reason for delay. It wanted nothing more than to see the straw castle burn, radiant as an atom bomb, and feel its skin-bubbling heat warm the late October air.

But I fought the firebug off and spent the evening calmly handing out candy to the neighborhood kids, wearing a Yoda mask and valiant in my self-denial.

This wasn't amateur hour.

We were going to do this shit right.

———

At midnight, long after the trick-or-treaters had stopped calling, I went up to my bedroom and put on gray cargo pants, a black sweater, a black stocking cap, and black hiking boots. I turned off the light and opened my bedroom door, cocking my head to listen to our silent house. Dad was definitely asleep—he'd gone to bed two hours earlier. Haylee was either asleep or watching something on her laptop with headphones on.

I went downstairs and left the house. The night was calm. Haylee's bedroom window was dark. My footsteps crunched on the driveway as I made my way to the Olds and opened its massive trunk. I took out my backpack, which was already packed for the mission, and softly shut the trunk. I headed down the driveway, turned left at the sidewalk, and went two blocks before stopping beneath a streetlight. After a minute or two, Katrina's black VW Bug pulled up in front of me. I opened the passenger door and slid in, setting the clinking backpack on my lap.

Katrina leaned over and kissed me. Colorful pops and fizzes filled my mind, darting frantically like water bugs.

"Hey," she said, pulling back. "You're dressed like a cat burglar."

"Burglary is for the greedy," I said, rubbing my tingling jaw. "Arson is for the pure of heart."

Katrina grinned and put the car in gear. The souped-up Bug rumbled as we rolled along.

"You have everything?"

I patted the bag on my lap, watching as far as the headlights reached. I felt as if an invisible hand were pushing me from behind, propelling me along. We left town on a county highway, turned onto the first crossroad, and circled back toward Hickson in a wide arc. We'd decided that parking in the Robinson lot, or anywhere in that neighborhood, was too obvious, especially if the Mayor or one of his cronies was on patrol. Instead, Katrina was going to drop me off north of the park and wait for me there. I'd need to drag myself through a half acre of scrubby woods and approach the castle from that direction. Luckily the castle was still lit up like a spaceship, even at two a.m. We could see it glowing from the road.

Katrina parked the car on the edge of the highway and turned off the headlights.

"You sure you don't want me to come with?"

"You're the getaway driver. The getaway driver gets to sit comfortably in the vehicle and smoke cigarettes."

"But you might need help."

"I appreciate that, but I work best alone."

Katrina smiled, a friendly ghost girl in the blue dashboard light. I reached out and gave her knee a squeeze.

"Jesus, Mack. This is crazy, you know?"

"Yeah, I guess."

"You're really going to do it?"

"Yes, ma'am."

"You don't have to do this if you don't want to. Don't do this to just, you know, impress me."

"I know."

Katrina unbuckled her seat belt. She leaned over and gave me another kiss. I copped a feel.

"All right, firebug," she whispered in my ear. "Go do your thing."

The woods bordering the park's north side were patchy but still dense enough to poke your eyes out if you weren't careful. I went slow, keeping my head down as I bumbled through, my hands extended to fend off branches and possible bear attacks. I hadn't brought a flashlight. This was a black-ops mission and all possible stealth was required. Grandpa Hedley had once told me about a friend of his in Vietnam who'd smoked a cigarette while on watch and gotten his head blown off by a sniper who'd spotted the cigarette's cherry.

"See, bucko," Grandpa Hedley had concluded, "smoking really will kill you."

Ha ha.

I didn't have a flashlight, but I did have the castle itself to guide me. All those floodlights trained on the two-story stack of straw bales had been installed with security in mind, no doubt, but they also happened to serve as a beacon, drawing me through the woods like a lanky mammoth. My eyes grew accustomed to the darkness and I got better at dodging trees, though I still got my fair amount of scratches. The closer I came to the castle, the brighter the forest around me became.

With perhaps fifty feet of woods left, I was startled by a smudge of color in the corner of my eye. When I turned, I saw only the base of an old tree with a fat, distended trunk. Like anybody else who'd grown up in Hickson, I thought immediately of Alfred James Hickson and wondered if it'd been a tree like this he'd tied himself to after getting bitten by that rabid raccoon. For all I knew, this was the tree itself—the official spot of Hickson's death had never been confirmed.

"Hello?" I whispered, feeling only half stupid. Ground leaves rustled and I continued forward, pushing away a serious case of the crawlies as I focused on the luminous structure ahead. More trees, more scraping branches. I reached the edge of the woods and crouched down, examining the scene.

A gap of ten open yards ran between the woods and Robinson Field. I was behind left field. The outfield wall was a regular chain-link fence, painted black and eight feet tall. Beyond the fence, about fifty additional feet distant, was the castle itself in all its flammable glory.

I unhooked the backpack from my shoulder and set it on the ground, dropping to my knees as I sifted through its contents. I took out my field binoculars, a birthday gift from Grandpa Hedley. I scanned Robinson Field for sentries but saw nothing but an empty baseball diamond. Nobody stood guard along the field's fence, drinking from a flask or smoking a night-watch cigarette. Nobody sat on the aluminum bleachers, whittling a walking stick to help pass the night's long hours.

If the park had been under guard earlier, it had been abandoned since. I now had two choices: I could prepare my little Molotov cocktails from the safety of the woods, chuck them over the outfield fence, and pray they hit castle, or else I could cross the exposed area, climb the fence, and run up to base of the castle itself, where I'd be able to start the burn at my leisure.

I eyed the distance between the outfield fence and the castle. I tried to imagine a bottle flying from my hand, covering all that distance, and landing at a suitable burn point. No, it was impossible. I was a string-bean man, with a string-bean arm. This would have to be up close and personal, a burn worthy of the great Firebug of Balrog County.

I zipped up the backpack, hooked its strap over my shoulder, and stood up. An owl hooted from deep inside the forest and I repressed an urge to hoot back. I ducked one last branch and stepped into the clearing. No searchlight snapped on to reveal me so I kept moving, keeping my head down as I ran to the outfield fence. I climbed that chain-link fucker in three seconds flat, dropped to the other side, and crossed the fifty feet to the rear of the castle, nestling up to it in a patch of darkness.

I sat back against the castle wall, a stitch forming in my side. I smelled dusty straw and freshly mown grass. The woods I'd just exited looked dark and wild and ominous, a place you wouldn't venture without a damn good reason.

I opened the backpack and took out three liquor bottles I'd filled with gasoline. The firebug zipped around my heart, ready to rock. I uncapped the bottles and the smell of gasoline instantly obliterated any scent of straw, grass, or anything else. I felt around the bag and pulled out the rags I was going to use as wicks. I doused a rag and stuffed it into the neck of the first bottle. This was it. The point of no—

Something whistled in the dark. A wooden stick appeared in the castle wall, about two feet from my head. I reached out and touched it, wondering if I'd started to hallucinate. The stick was smooth except for a trio of feathers on its rear end.

An arrow.

It was a motherfucking arrow.

I turned and peered into the night. A patch of grass in deep right field was moving toward the castle—a man done up in full jungle camo, carrying a high-tension recurve bow.

Instantly terrified, I chucked the liquor bottle in his general direction and hustled toward the left-field fence, leaving the backpack and my beautiful dream of haunted castle hellfire behind.

I sprinted at top speed, my long, bony legs churning beneath me. I didn't duck my head, didn't think. I just ran like hell, ignoring the whistling of additional arrows tearing through the night sky. I was the wind. I was the wind shot out of a cannon.

My eyes watered as I reached the warning track. I leapt onto the chain-link wall one-two-three and I was on the other side. An arrow clanged off the fencing. I swore and sprinted for the woods. I made it about five feet past the tree line before I tripped over a root and plunged face first into a mound of dirt. I rolled over and leapt to my feet, swatting at my face and chest.

I'd fallen into an ant hill. Fire ants, and damn if they weren't bitey.

An arrow plunged into the ground at my feet. I swore again and stumbled deeper into the woods. When I looked back through the trees, I saw the camo man climbing the outfield fence. He'd swung his bow around his shoulder and was moving with stiff certainty, an old timer who could still hump it when he needed to.

I wanted to shout something, something taunting and obscene, but I knew camo man would recognize my voice and then I'd be screwed no matter how fast I got through the woods. I could hear my own breathing, loud and obvious, and wondered if I'd finally gone insane. Was this wooded chase actually happening? Had my grandfather really spent the entire night lying on his stomach in Robinson Field? Did that make him crazy, too? Was our entire damn family crazy? Would a mental health expert suggest group therapy, individual therapy, or a mix of the two?

The sound of motivated branch-snapping grew louder behind me. I picked up the pace and prayed my feet wouldn't betray me a second time. I expected an arrow in the back at any moment but still believed this was preferable to being found out—the crestfallen look I could expect from my grandmother when she learned of my degenerate tendencies. Those big, milky blue eyes, all sad and disappointed.

No. I would keep running. I would risk impalement. The firebug and I had not come this far to pussy out now.

I pushed through a hundred branches and endured a hundred cuts. At long last, I emerged from the woods and stepped onto the county road, which ran straight and true like a blacktop river. I saw no car waiting for me. I saw only a dark road, in the middle of a dark night, and heard more branches snapping in the woods behind me.

I was lost. Forsaken.

An engine rumbled to life and headlights lit up the road. It was Katrina's Bug, having apparently disabled its cloaking mechanism. I raised my hand to shield my dazzled eyes and the Bug roared toward me. I hunched my shoulders and thought small thoughts. When the car finally reached me, slowing but not stopping, I flung open the passenger door and leapt inside, shouting GO-GO-GO like a bank robber in a movie.

Katrina stepped on the gas and the Bug lurched forward, eager to fly. I glanced in the rearview mirror and saw the camo man step onto the road, his hunting bow slung over his shoulder.

"Fuck," Katrina shouted, her long black hair whipping in the wind. "What happened?"

Camo man grew smaller in the mirror, then receded into the night altogether.

"I ran into an unexpected impediment," I said. "The mission had to be aborted."

Katrina glanced at me and frowned. I looked down at my scratched forearms, the cut lines gummy blue in the dashboard light. Disappointment filled the car like an invisible yet poisonous gas and I could feel Katrina growing distant even as she remained seated beside me. In the brief span of twenty minutes, I'd gone from lovable local renegade to just another loser who'd let her down. Not only had the firebug failed, failed like a scared little bitch, but it had also been identified by a man who did not take such transgressions lightly.

I leaned back in my seat as we hurtled through the night. A new and terrible darkness had fallen upon the land.

Letter to the Editor

Dear Editor,

Do you ever feel sad? Does your heart ever ache inside your chest with longing and despondency at the ephemeral nature of existence? It's your old pal the Firebug here (if you had not already guessed this from receiving yet another piece of anonymous mail slipped carefully beneath your door).

Yes, sir, I guess I was feeling down tonight and just wanted to write you a letter. I think we've achieved something like friendship these past weeks, you the editor and I the mysterious contributor, so I hope you'll feel somewhat saddened to know this will be my last missive.

Yep, you heard me! I am retiring from the editorial letter business and perhaps from starting fires as well. You know what they say: if you play with fire long enough, eventually somebody will shoot at you with a high-tension bow.

Sincerely,
The Firebug

The Firebug Wakes

On the day we took Mom off life support, I stayed up watching TV until two a.m. I was the only one in the house still awake, which felt strange because my mother was normally up at all hours, catching what sleep she could in small increments, like a cat. I turned on a lamp and examined our living room. I was in the presence of a multitude of Mom-based items. Her slippers peeked out from beneath the coffee table. Her spare eyeglasses sat on the end table beside me. Her box of tissues was by my feet. Her favorite quilt was bunched against my hip.

I stood up. Her books were in the built-in bookshelves; her favorite paintings were hanging on the walls. She'd gotten Dad to paint the living room a weird deep blue. She'd picked out the couch and chosen the cool blue and white striped fabric to reupholster it with.

But these weren't really items anymore.

They were artifacts.

My back tightened and my shoulders sunk inward. I took a deep breath, held it until I saw fizzy dots, and let it out slowly. I left the living room and headed down to the basement.

Our basement was cold and cobwebby, outlaw territory. It flooded occasionally, so the floor was simply painted concrete and chilly to the touch even in the summertime—if you had a troubled mind, you could pace around it for hours without making any floorboards creak. The two biggest rooms were the rec room and the laundry room, with the other two used for storage and spider hoarding. We still had a coal chute in the laundry room, from back in the day when they'd deliver coal for your furnace right to your house. We also had a crappy weight bench in the corner of the rec room where you could reel off a few sets when you felt pissed off.

Tonight, I'd come to the basement to pace and grieve without worrying about waking my father and sister. Yes, here I had come to feel my skin grow heated, my eyes puffy, and my chest hitch as the initial wave of what had occurred that day, and its utter permanence, finally rolled over me.

Ah, such sob-choked lamentations.

Even the spiders let me be.

———————

Two days passed. I ate a lot of cheese-based casseroles, Dad drank a lot of beer, and Haylee existed on oxygen and sleep. Flowers and gift baskets arrived from all over. Our family had achieved a kind of temporary local celebrity status—we were in mourning for a woman who'd died too young.

She leaves behind two children and a loving husband.
That kind of business.

On the evening of Mom's wake, we piled into the van and drove to the mortuary. Grandpa and Grandma Hedley were already there, standing outside the mortuary's entrance despite the chilly November day. "We can see her first," Grandma Hedley said, ushering us inside. "Before the official viewing begins."

We took off our coats in a long hallway and hung them on wooden hangers. Grandpa Hedley led the way into the viewing room, which was lit in soft white light and smelled like lavender and old man cologne. Short, padded chairs had been placed around the edges of the room, chairs for sitting and chatting, and a casket sat up front, the room's dominant centerpiece.

Haylee glided toward the casket while the rest of us hung back.

"He does good work," Grandpa Hedley said, touching the knot on his tie. "I've always said he does good work."

Grandma Hedley smiled and squeezed my hand. Dad looked from the casket to the floor and back to the casket.

"I appreciate you arranging things, May," he said, his voice a hoarse whisper. "You too, George. Thank you for your help."

Grandpa Hedley coughed into his hand and cleared his throat, embarrassed by all this display from his son-in-law. He looked toward the hall doorway and hitched up his leather belt.

I joined my sister by the casket.

"Jesus," I said.

"I know, right?"

"She never wore that much makeup in her entire life."

"And what's with that lipstick? Who wears bright pink '80s lipstick anymore?"

I closed my eyes and rubbed them until I saw colors. This tarted-up corpse was both our mother and very much not our mother. This was our mother when Haylee was five years old and allowing Haylee to use her as a makeup doll.

"What should we do? Should we say something?"

I opened my eyes and the painted version of our mother was still there. Chest not rising, hands folded over in that way she liked to sleep on the couch. That way we always joked about because it made her look dead.

"I don't think we can do anything, Haystack. The viewing is about to start."

Haylee didn't say anything.

"It'll be okay."

I took my sister's small hand and gave it a squeeze. I could feel the eyes of my father and grandparents upon us, waiting for a sign to come forward.

"I didn't feel anything," Haylee said. "When she died."

"What do you mean?"

"Like, her soul. I didn't feel her soul leave her body. I didn't feel her get called up to heaven or whatever."

Mom was wearing mascara, I realized. It added some David Bowie to her open casket look. A little glam.

"You'd think if anybody would go to heaven, it'd be her, right? That we'd be able to feel her leaving?"

I let go of Haylee's hand. "Yeah. I guess so."

Grandpa Hedley cleared his throat and I knew we had company, that the mortuary dude and his mortuary wife had entered the room. Soon a line of locals would shuffle on in, view my mother's gussied-up corpse, and offer their condolences. Sam would show up with his grandma, dressed in his black Johnny Cash suit, and later we'd walk to my house together, not saying much, and proceed to get drunk in the basement on a pilfered three-liter bottle of condolence wine. We'd get so hammered I wouldn't remember Sam helping me to bed and I'd wake up in my own dried vomit the next day, having dreamt of my mother visiting me inside an otherwise black abyss, grown ten feet tall and painted like a clown, looming before me like Frankenstein's monster, and, even looking like that, my dream self would be so glad to see her. I would beg for her to say anything, anything at all, but she would retreat into that abyss without having uttered a sound.

But right at that moment, all that fun stuff lay ahead of me. I could only put my arm around my sister, utter some banal reassurance, and wait while the rest of the world stepped up for a view.

———

I volunteered to deliver my mother's eulogy. I'd done a paper on Pericles' funeral oration in English class and figured I'd be able to do my mother justice. Anything would be better than relying on the church's pastor, who'd lived in Hickson for only two years and whom I'd never even met.

However, I hadn't counted on the enormous bottle of wine I'd shared with Sam the night before and the massive hangover it had wrought. I also hadn't expected the preacher to repeatedly tell me that if delivering the eulogy got to be too much for me, I could sit down and he'd step up to help finish it. Up until that point, I hadn't factored in the emotion that would pour through me as I spoke about my mother. I'd figured my mother needed a eulogy so I'd give her a fucking eulogy. I'd be damned if I was going to break down MID-EULOGY AND LET THE GODDAMN PREACHER FINISH WHAT I HAD STARTED.

Thus I was filled with a strange mixture of hangover pain, prideful rage, and determination when I finally did deliver my mother's speech, sputtering and half-choked with sorrow. I led off with three quotes we'd taped above her hospital bed on a sheet of printer paper, talked about how much good work she'd done and how well she'd handled her terrible fucking illnesses, and then I rambled to some kind of conclusion about how much we'd all miss her.

All in all, it wasn't my best work. It was a sad speech given by a sad fifteen-year-old kid in a suit coat he'd borrowed from his father only to find the sleeves two inches too short for his long and spindly arms. A serviceable speech, perhaps, but nothing like the glowing red-hot gem

265

of brilliance my mother deserved, a woman whose life had so obviously earned a two-week period of feasting and gladiatorial games and not some lame church service and a speedy trip to the crematorium. A speech, honestly, I am internally rewriting to this day and will probably rewrite until I croak myself.

———————

I skipped the post-funeral ham sandwich chit-chat and walked home alone. I tried not to think about how my mother, coffin and all, was being delivered at that very moment to the crematorium in Thorndale, where she'd be reduced to a few pounds of ashy soot and poured into a cardboard urn. When I opened the door to our house, the smell of flowers was so pungent it made my eyes water and caused my thoughts to detach in a strange, floating way. I found myself standing in my parents' bedroom. I looked around. I felt coolly objective, like a burglar casing a mansion.

An idea bubbled in my mind. I passed through the remodeled bathroom and entered my mother's laundry room/walk-in closet. The two robes she'd worn during her long sickness, one terry cloth and the other silk, were hanging beside the blouses and pantsuits she'd worn to work. I pulled the robes off their hangers and carried them out to the living room, where I dropped them on the couch. I followed her oxygen hose back to its base and detached it from HAL. I wound the tubing into a bundle and tossed that onto the couch along with her box of tissues, her prescription medication, and her favorite couch pillow. I went down to the basement, found the box of her medical bills (paperwork my father liked to pore over at the kitchen table like a lawyer before a big case) and brought the box up to the couch. Finally, I searched the house and retrieved two dozen inspirational books, gooey reams of happy-happy bullshit people had given to Mom. I added those to the pile as well.

The mound of terrible was impressive. I got a lawn bag out from beneath the kitchen sink, dumped all the terrible inside of it, and hoisted the bag over my shoulder like a skinny, hung-over Santa Claus.

"Ho, ho, ho," I wheezed, shifting the heavy bag on my shoulder. I went back into the kitchen, paused long enough to grab a book of matches from the junk drawer, and went out through the back door. The air was fresher in the backyard, less pungent with gift basket flower smell. I trundled across the backyard and into the woods, burrowing forward until I came to the first open space hidden from the house, a treeless patch Haylee and I called the Spot. The Spot was good for hiding and exchanging secrets. The Spot was good for daytime camping, snow-fort building, and, as you got older, smoking and drinking with friends.

Most of the recent snow had melted, leaving the Spot brown and ugly and damp. I dropped the bag of terrible from my shoulder and spilled its contents into the Spot's center. I overturned the box of medical bills, crumpled several sheets of paper into fire-friendly balls, and placed them strategically around the Mound of Terrible's base.

Still, I was not convinced. I went back toward the house, nabbed a can of lighter fluid from the garage, and returned to the Spot. I doused the whole heap with fluid until the can squeezed dry and then I chucked that onto the pile, too.

"Goodbye, terrible things."

The pile caught on the third match, a pleasant *WHUMP* that caused me to step backward into an evergreen. The bills, the books, the robes, even the plastic oxygen tubing began to burn. My heart went bump in my chest and sent a short, manic burst of joy through my body, the first truly good thing I'd felt in a week.

For the first time, the firebug had truly woken.

A Cow to Slaughter

I woke early on Monday morning, fuzzy-headed and exhausted. The sound of arrows whistling past my head had filled my dreams and my soul was heavy with dread. The idea that my own grandfather had somehow not recognized me seemed as ridiculous as the failed assault on the haunted castle itself—George Hedley was a canny Vietnam vet, a mayor with thirty years experience, and a kick-ass hunter to boot. Shit. He cared so much about catching the county's mystery arsonist that he'd hid in the cold and dewy grass past midnight. And he was fucking seventy-two!

I went to school like a cow to slaughter. I spent each class period staring at various white boards, a tunnel of howling darkness swirling around me. I waited for my name to be called over the intercom or a SWAT team to come crashing in through the windows. At lunch, I could only stare at my food while the lunchroom buzzed around me.

"Don't you like Italian dunkers anymore?"

I flinched. I'd forgotten Sam was sitting across from me, happily chowing down on his own lunch.

"I like dunkers fine."

"Then why aren't you eating them?"

"I'm not hungry."

"You're always hungry. You're like a tapeworm with wacky blond hair."

"Really, Sam. I don't know what to say that."

"You always know what to say to everything. Are you sick? Did you fucking party last night without me?"

I picked up one of the pieces of cheesy bread and dunked it in the marinara sauce. I stuck it in my mouth and chewed, giving it the old high school cafeteria try. It tasted like a lump of glue.

"Sam," I said, swallowing with difficulty. "I'm not the upstanding citizen you think I am."

Sam drank his chocolate milk and eyed my tray.

"Good," he said. "I hate upstanding citizens."

I looked across the table. Good old Sam, I thought. Good old low moral standards, Orson Wells–looking Sam Chervenik. He'd understand when they came for me in the dark of night and hauled me off to big boy jail. He'd go to my trial. He knew about the kind of darkness a firebug could be born into.

"I don't know anymore, Sam. Life is terrifying. Life is out to attack you."

"Blah blah blah. Are you going to eat or not?"

I handed over the untouched dunker to Sam and pushed my lunch tray away. There was no point in reasoning with the lad. He'd learn in time.

Camo man, camo man. Where art thou?

Sharpening my knives, little buggy.

Sharpening my knives.

Big Greg took off when I showed up after school so Hickson Hardware was a one-man operation for the afternoon. We'd received a delivery of snow shovels, snow blowers, and ice salt earlier that day. November had begun and Balrog County's annual six months of frozen fuck-all was on the horizon. The squirrels were fat, the deer were uneasy, and the rickety old men were ready to bitch and moan about our slippery parking lot until spring.

I stocked the new merch and tried not to cringe every time somebody entered the store. I'd be surprised if Grandpa Hedley took a direct approach—an obvious assault wasn't really his style. He'd come at me sideways. Probably get his buddies on the police force involved, do something to scare me straight.

The door chimed at four, waking me from a light doze at the front counter. I lifted my head and wiped the drool off my cheek as Katrina entered the store and stopped, silhouetted by the sunlight outside.

"Hey there, slacker."

I slid off my stool and stood up. "Hey."

Katrina approached the counter. She was wearing her black leather jacket and a purple infinity scarf.

"Busy today, huh?"

"Yep. One of those manic Mondays."

Katrina looked around. I leaned forward and saw the hardware store the way she must have seen it: dull and silent and three steps toward the grave.

"You need more hacksaw blades? I've got an employee discount."

"No, I'm good. Actually, I'm losing interest in that project."

"Really? The birdhouses?"

"I don't know. I went down to the basement this morning and they just seemed ... sad, you know? All those dead skeleton birds, chilling in their empty little houses."

"Yeah. I think they're really cool."

Katrina stuck her hands in her back pockets and rocked on her heels. "I don't know. I guess I don't care so much about cool anymore."

"You don't?"

Katrina shrugged. "Where's cool really get you, anyway?"

"Into the best dance clubs in America, that's where."

The wind gusted outside, rattling the hardware store's windows. I leaned back and crossed my arms.

"So, why the surprise visit? Avoiding studying?

Katrina pulled a car magazine off the front rack and started flipping through it. "Oh, you know. I guess I just found myself out walking and thought I'd stop by. There's not a lot of destinations in Hickson to really aim for."

"You missed me, didn't you?"

Katrina rolled her eyes, trying to repress a little smile.

"You did, didn't you? You needed yourself a little Mack fix."

"Please," Katrina said, dropping the magazine back on the shelf. "You're going to make me puke."

"Puke with love."

"Shit."

Katrina gave me a healthy shove and I flailed backward, almost tripping over the register stool. As she marched out of the store, regally tossing her dark ringletted hair, I realized the visit had been her way of saying the haunted castle fuck-up was all right, that she still dug me whether I was a successful firebug or not.

Katrina wasn't in it for the burn.

She was in it for me.

———————

Fifteen minutes before closing time, two fire trucks and a police car roared past the store, sirens blaring. I stepped out onto the sidewalk and watched as seventy-five percent of Hickson's emergency responders headed east. A substantial plume of black smoke rose in the distance.

My cell phone buzzed in my pocket. Sam.

"Yo."

"You won't believe this, dude. Somebody torched the straw castle."

"What?"

"I'm over here right now. I was on my afternoon walk-about."

"The haunted castle's on fire?"

"Yeah, it's like the end of *The Wicker Man* over here.

You should come check it out. I'm guessing this baby's going to burn for a couple hours, easy."

Somebody shouted in Sam's background. Sirens blared.

"Is my grandpa there?"

"I don't know. Maybe. There's a shit ton of people here. It's like a disaster party."

I squinted, keeping the phone to my ear. The amount of black smoke on the horizon was definitely increasing.

"I think I'm going to pass on the fire, Sammy Boy."

"What? Are you serious?"

"Yes, Sam," I said, wincing. "I have never been so serious."

I ended the call. The firebug was wide awake and flipping out but I still remembered the feeling of dread I'd woken up with that morning. This burn felt like a setup, another move to literally smoke me out of hiding.

I went back into the store and turned out the lights, deciding to let Big Greg add up the register in the morning. I just wanted to go home, burrow beneath my comforter, and get some goddamn rest for once. I started home, lost in warm and fuzzy Katrina-type thoughts and feeling the approach of winter in the air.

A block from our house, I realized the crackling I'd been hearing wasn't acorns popping beneath my feet, and that the smell of smoke in the air was coming from much closer than Robinson Park.

Our house was on fire.

The Reckoning

This wasn't some kitchen grease fire. This was an all-encompassing blaze that had already reached the second story of our house and begun to lick at the roof, an incandescent, white-hot scorcher I could feel on my skin. I started running, stupidly penetrating deeper into the heat, but I had to pull up thirty feet short, blinded by the sweat in my eyes. Nothing short of a tidal wave was going to stop this burn. Whatever was still inside our house wasn't making it out.

I stumbled on my heels, reeling from the heat, and stepped onto the grassy edge of the ravine that separated our yard from the train tracks.

"Not as fun when it's yours going up, is it?"

I wiped the sweat from my eyes and turned around. Ox Haggerton was standing on the far side of the ravine. Dressed oddly in denim coveralls and rubber hip waders, his nose was bright red and his blue eyes were unnaturally bright. He had a rifle casually propped on one shoulder and held it like a man so accustomed to its weight that he didn't notice it.

"Damn, boy. You should see the look on your face right now."

Our living room's bay window detonated, an explosion of glass and belching flame that rolled onto the front porch. My tongue felt stuffed and heavy in my mouth and I wondered if I was dreaming. One of those nightmares where you can't move, or move too slow for it to matter.

My writing journal.

My books.

All my beautiful books.

"Don't worry," Ox said, grinning. "Your people aren't inside."

He leaned over and spat chewing tobacco. Haylee and Dad, I realized, would still be in Thorndale, attending her afternoon therapy session.

"Our dog," I said. "Was he still in there?"

Ox wiped his nose with his sleeve and bore into me with his crazy blue eyes.

"You folks had a dog?"

"Chompy. He could have been in his kennel. In the basement."

"What the hell kind of name is Chompy?"

A window exploded on the second story. Haylee's bedroom.

"He was a good dog."

"I bet." Ox toed the ground with his boot. "Well, shit. I don't think dogs really count as murder, do they?"

I took a step down the slope, toward Ox. He lifted the rifle off his shoulder and held it in both hands.

"You shouldn't have come out to my place, son. None of this would be happening if you'd respected my property."

"Maybe not, Ox, but you'd still be an asshole nobody can stand."

Haggerton's mouth tightened into a knot. I still didn't hear any sirens, distant or otherwise.

"You're wondering where the cavalry is," Haggerton said. "Well, the whole damn neighborhood took off to go watch that ugly straw heap burn in the park. You should have seen them all peeling out of here, like flies to shit. I guess we ain't the only ones who appreciate a good fire."

"You started that one, too."

"You got it, kid. Thought I'd finish what you couldn't."

"And that was you hiding in the outfield."

Haggerton chuckled and spat more chew. "Last night was as much fun as I've had in years. When you climbed over that outfield fence I recognized you straight off as Hedley's grandkid and hunted you for the hell of it. Almost had you, too, but I hadn't figured on a getaway driver. Usually shitbags like you work alone."

I turned to watch the fire, deciding I didn't care whether the old coot shot me in the back or not. The fire had eaten through the roof in patches, exposing the building's innards to the blackened sky. My parents had purchased the house before I was born, right when they'd gotten married. That made for twenty years of Druneswald occupancy, more or less.

I noticed smoke coming from the garage. The garage

door was rolled up and a healthy fire was roaring, right where my car was usually parked—

"Motherfuck."

I sprinted up the driveway, seized with a fresh wave of crazed wildness. I heard a crack and a patch of gravel in front of me kicked up dust. I pulled up.

"No, no," Haggerton shouted from across the ravine. "You come back here, asshole. I'm not done talking to you."

I turned around, my eyes and throat aching. The heat had sucked all the moisture from the world.

"You lit my car on fire."

"That's right," Haggerton said, nodding. "Right after I found the bullet dent on your trunk. It was a little bitch, all right, but I know a bullet dent when I see one. Particularly one made by my own rifle."

A whistle blew south of town. Not an ambulance or a fire truck. Just a train, passing through Hickson like this was any other day. I wondered if the conductor could see our house smoking in the distance and what he made of it from his perch in the engine. More likely, he was watching the heavy plume of smoke on the east side of town along with everyone else.

Haggerton scratched his chin with the stock of his rifle.

"So what, kid, you think because your mama kicked the bucket, that makes you special? That you can just do whatever the fuck you want, valuable personal property be damned? You think you're the only one who ever lost somebody?"

"How about you go fuck yourself, Ox."

"Oh yeah?"

"Yeah."

Ox Haggerton clicked off his rifle's safety and aimed it at my chest, nestling the gun into his shoulder. The sound of the roaring fire behind me, as well as every other sound in the world, dropped away. I peered down the barrel of Haggerton's rifle and saw nothing but a long, dark descent I probably had coming.

The ground shook as the train approached. Something inside our house exploded.

Ox Haggerton lowered his rifle.

"All right. I'm not going to kill you, boy. We're settled, far as I'm concerned."

The train blew its whistle again, a deep and primal noise the rumbled in my gut. Haggerton set his rifle back on his shoulder, turned around, and crossed the railroad tracks in two fluid strides as he headed for the woods beyond. The train roared out from behind the tree line, all thunder and sparks, and by the time it'd blown through, Old Man Haggerton had vanished into legend.

The Face of God

Across town, nearly everyone in Hickson watched the straw castle burn. Later they would speak of its white, incandescent flame in deeply reverent tones, as if they'd seen the face of God and somehow lived to talk about it.

Sam said you had to be there.

The Great Conflagration

The Great Conflagration lasted for three days, blotting out the sky and sending the citizens of Balrog County scrambling for safety. Not only had Ox Haggerton set fires on both sides of Hickson, but he'd begun his busy afternoon by igniting a blaze in the woods five miles north of town. This carefully executed trio of burns was a masterwork of arson that put my entire firebug career to shame. Yes, the grumpy old fucker had put one more snot-nosed kid in his place before skipping town.

A warrant had been put out for Ox Haggerton's arrest and all eyes were turned toward him now, believing Haggerton responsible for all the recent fires, but I still could not shake a feeling of vague uneasiness. I told the authorities about my encounter with Haggerton in my driveway but omitted my own role in cultivating his rage. Unable to stand the soft, periodic weeping of my sister, who mourned her puppy's kennel-trapped death above all, I spent long periods outside, alone in my grandparents' backyard, wrapped in heavy blankets as I watched helicopters fitted with buckets work endlessly, dumping load after load of water they'd collected from a nearby lake. I felt like a character in Thomas Mann's *The Magic Mountain*, listlessly taking the cure for consumption in a smoky version of the Swiss Alps. I belonged in the cluttered Grotto now and I wouldn't leave it for the rest of my life. Grandma Hedley would bring me food, I'd endure the harsh winter cold, and never would I light a fire or harm a single creature, great or small, ever again.

I kept picturing Old Man Haggerton, standing stiff and ready and trying to decide if I was worth shooting.

That look in his eyes.

––––––––––

On Wednesday, the Conflagration's third afternoon, Grandpa Hedley came out to the Grotto with a cup of coffee and sat down beside me in one of the patio chairs. He and my grandmother had been working nonstop since the fires, helping out with various town emergency-type things, and so I hadn't seen him much. His clothes were blackened by soot and ash and he smelled like he'd stepped directly out of a campfire. When he sat down beside me I turned my head away and stared at the Grotto's statue of Michelangelo, examining it like I'd never seen a big dangling stone penis before.

Grandpa Hedley made soft slurping sounds as he drank his coffee. He leaned back and considered the smoke-hazed sky.

"She got out of hand, didn't she?"

I glanced at my grandfather. Clearly sleep-deprived, he looked so tired and old I could hardly stand it.

"Yeah," I said, unsure of exactly what he was getting at. "She sure did."

Nobody said anything for a minute and my grandfather sipped his coffee like he had all the time in the world. It was cold as hell out, but he was just wearing a long-sleeved denim shirt with the sleeves rolled up. The shirt had a POW logo stitched onto the breast pocket.

Grandpa Hedley sat forward and cupped his hands around his coffee mug.

"I should have nipped it all in the bud, I suppose."

I licked my lips, which were painfully cracked and dry from the past three days of sitting outside.

"Nipped what in the bud?"

Grandpa Hedley sighed and waved a hand at the gray sky.

"Your firebug hobby. Our little cat-and-mouse game."

I leaned forward in my chair and stared at the space between my knees. I noticed that the Grotto's concrete patio was rife with cracks, some big enough for weeds to poke through. Even the most cared-for place in town was sliding toward ruin.

"You mean Haggerton's firebug hobby, don't you?"

"No, Mack. I know it was you, setting those earlier fires. Hell, you really expect me to believe Ox burned down his own wood pile? The man loved that wood pile beyond all reason. You set those early fires, Mack, and then you set off

Haggerton like a firecracker. Why else would he pick your house for his grand finale?"

Grandpa Hedley sipped his coffee. The world had grown even colder and I could feel it pressing down on me like the lid of a coffin. The jig was up. The screw had turned.

"Actually, I figured it was you ever since that second letter you wrote to the *Herald*'s editor. Nobody else around here writes like that." Grandpa Hedley patted my knee. "Shit. Nobody else around here is like you, Mack."

I felt my throat swell and threaten to choke me. I grabbed it and tried to massage the lump.

"Then why didn't you call the cops on me? Or tell me to stop?"

Grandpa Hedley shrugged. "I figured you were working through something you needed to get out of your system. Some type of poison. I looked at the burns first-hand and decided you weren't out to hurt anybody. If I'd gone to the police, you'd already turned eighteen and it might have meant jail time and a rough future. If I'd warned you off directly, you might not have listened or you might have quit and eventually drowned in that poison. I've known a lot of troubled young men over the years, Mack. They don't all make it."

I quit massaging my throat. The lump wasn't going away anytime soon.

"Of course, I didn't predict Haggerton going wild over one old woodpile," my grandfather continued, "but I suppose old Ox is as clear a case of a poisoned man as you'll ever see. You're too young to remember this, Mack, but Ox's wife left him back in the '80s, after they had a third miscarriage and zero kids. He turned mean after that and fell into the bottle."

I turned to my grandfather. "Do you want me to give myself up? I will. You can bring me in yourself."

Grandpa Hedley shook his head. "No. I considered it, but I don't see how that'll serve anyone now. You've learned your lesson about starting your little fires, haven't you?"

"Yes, sir," I said, shuddering under my cocoon of blankets. "I have and I am truly sorry."

"I thought you might be, sitting out here like this." Grandpa Hedley turned and looked back at the house. "It's not a pleasant thing to hear your sister crying like that, is it?"

"No," I said, feeling the knot in my throat swell even more. "It's not."

We listened for a moment but I couldn't hear anything but the wind blowing through the Grotto. Sometimes Haylee would run out of crying and need to drink some water for a couple of minutes. She'd begun to remind me of the professional mourners you could hire in the Far East, the ones really good at keening.

"Well," Grandpa Hedley said, turning back around in his chair. "I'm not saying I'm as innocent as Mary here either, kid. You know, I was enjoying our little covert war. The letters in the newspaper and the sneaking around. It was fun. It got me amped up for the first time in a long while and I liked it. I may be an old man playing at mayor, but I'm no angel myself. I used to kick around some."

I stared at my grandfather and imagined him as a young

man. A young man running around Vietnam with grenades and a knife and an assault rifle. A young man who'd done that and saw all that and then come back home again to sit quietly behind a desk and raise a family.

"But you're going to do one thing for me, Mack."

I raised my head. Anything, I thought. Anything the fuck you want.

"You're going to tell your father exactly what you've been up to. You owe the man that much."

The Pit

By Thursday afternoon the Great Conflagration was considered under control, if not totally out. Dad and I convinced Haylee to come with us to see if we could salvage anything from the house. The police had cordoned off the last two blocks of our street and we had to park the van on a side street. When we stepped outside it felt as if we were astronauts landing on a strange and possibly hostile planet. The burnt smell was stronger here, like bacon charred in a cast-iron skillet.

We went up half a block and turned onto our street, stepping around the traffic sawhorses.

"Holy shit," Haylee said.

We stopped and took in the scene. As reported, the homes on the street's north side were in various states of ruin while all the south side homes appeared untouched except for a heavy coating of soot, as if a protective force field in the middle of the street had deflected all flame. It was like something out of the Old Testament, a Passover of fire. I noticed lights on in the south houses, a curtain pulled back.

We walked on. Two of our neighbors were already poking through their own wreckage, heads down as they scowled at what they found. Dad waved, but they didn't notice us.

"This is why you pay those premiums," Dad said, cramming his hands into the pockets of his new jacket. "Just look at this mess. One lunatic decides to go off and you get all this."

The last three houses on the street, including ours, had burned to their foundations. Our basement, now exposed to the sky, was a murky pit of charred trash and dirty water. An unlucky red squirrel had fallen into the mess and now lay floating among the debris, his little belly a spot of white amid the dark.

Haylee walked away from us and began to circle our house's foundation, slowly picking her way through the rubble. Our garage was gone and the blackened metal shell of my Oldsmobile was clearly visible. The scene reminded me of old footage from bombed-out war zones like Beirut or Dresden. The forest that had once surrounded our neighborhood was now a field of skeletal wreckage with a scorched train track running along its edge. A dead forest that went on for miles.

Dad blew into his hands. It was a cold day and you could smell snow mixed with the burnt.

"Your mother loved this house so much," Dad said. "This would have killed her all over again."

I stared at the floating squirrel. My heart felt hollowed

out. The firebug was either dead or had gone far, far underground. The game was over and in it I would find solace no more. I would apply to college. I would force myself into the wide world and get along as best I could.

That would be my penance.

"Dad," I said, raising my head. "I was the one who set fire to Ox Haggerton's woodpile. I burned down Teddy Giles' boathouse, too."

My father turned to look at me. I watched as trusting, stir-fry-cooking Pete Druneswald realized what had been under his nose all this time. The devil he'd harbored on the second floor.

"Haggerton chose our house because of me. He figured out what I did and wanted revenge."

I pictured a prisoner standing before a firing squad and smoking one last cigarette, bravely awaiting his fate with open eyes.

"I'm sorry, Dad. I didn't think this would get so out of hand. I was just trying to have some fun."

My father pursed his lips, his face flushing red. A sharp north wind gusted through the dead forest and bits of ash fluttered around us like snowflakes.

"You selfish ... jerk."

"I'm sorry."

"You selfish ... little ... snot."

"I know—"

Dad stepped forward, his chest puffing out. "You *know*? What do you know, Mack? Do you know how frightened she was before they put her under sedation? Before they shoved those tubes down her throat?"

Dad shoved me in the chest. I staggered back, surprised.

"No, you don't know, do you? Because you weren't there, Mack. You missed her leaving us because you wanted to do what you wanted to do. You had to take that stupid history test. You always have to have your way. You're willful. You're a willful little jerk."

Dad shoved me again, but I was ready for it this time and stood my ground. I could feel my sister watching us from across the basement pit, her eyes like twin black holes absorbing it all for later, for the rest of her life.

"She asked for you, Mack. Did Haylee ever tell you? Your mother was scared and she asked and you weren't there."

I shuddered and bowed my head as a cold wind blew through me. I took a step back, and then another. I could feel the watery pit looming at my heels, dirty and disgusting and shallow—the kind of place I belonged. I let my body go loose and pitched backward.

As I fell, I could hear my sister scream and a train rumble through my mind. I hit the water first and the basement's concrete floor second, knocking my tailbone and the back of my head before I bobbed up again.

Colorful sparks dotted my vision.

The water was cold enough to stop your heart.

Haylee called my name. She ran around the edge of the pit and stood beside my father, who was bent over at the waist with his hands upon his knees, like he'd been sucker punched. She was crying. He was crying. They called my name. And then, lo, a bony creature appeared beside them, himself filthy with soot and ash. A creature freshly returned from the shadowlands, from Mordor. He barked and wagged his scraggly tail, irrepressible as a son-of-a-bitch, and I knew he, too, was calling my name.

One Last Burn

The next day, sore as hell but still in one piece, I drove to Katrina's house to escape my brooding family for a few hours. Although Chompy had returned to us (a little hungry but otherwise fine), relations between my family and I were understandably tense. I felt exhausted and hollowed out and didn't know if I could handle feeling any more goddamn emotions. I just wanted to sleep for a thousand days and magically wake up back in my old house and for everyone to be happy and not totally pissed off at me for being such a degenerate.

Katrina was waiting for me out on her lawn. She had her hair tied back in a workmanlike ponytail and wasn't wearing any makeup, not even her trusty mascara. When she smiled and waved at me I felt like dropping to my knees and falling on a sword, I was so grateful.

Then she did something even crazier—she hugged me in broad daylight.

"That's so crazy about your dog. I'm glad he's okay."

"Yeah," I said. "I am too."

"Haylee must have been so happy."

"Yeah. She was."

Katrina took my hand and pulled me along. "Okay. I have something for you, Mack-Attack."

"Is it sex? Because I don't think I can handle sex right now. I mean, either physically or mentally."

"No. It's even better than sex."

"Whoa," I said, allowing her to lead me across the lawn. "This I need to see."

We went around the back of her house to the fire pit, which was loaded with wooden boxes that had been stacked in a loose pyramid. I looked at Katrina, then again at the boxes. Katrina squeezed my hand and grinned.

"It's the birdhouses."

"Your birdhouses?"

"Yep. All of them."

I stepped closer to the fire pit. "But you love your birdhouses. They're your dark therapy."

"Yeah, but I don't think I need them anymore." Katrina whipped out a box of matches from her pocket and slapped it onto my palm. "I thought we could do one last burn together before you go straight. You know. For good luck."

I stared into the fire pit. Crushed balls of newspaper had been stuffed around its base with loving care.

"What happened to the bird skeletons?"

"I buried them," Katrina said, pointing to the patch of freshly churned dirt in the garden. "Along with a copy of *Jonathan Livingston Seagull*."

I smiled at this brilliant touch and opened the box of

matches. I took a single stick out and held it up, studying its phosphorus-gelatin head.

Katrina leaned in and gave me a kiss. "Light'er up, dude."

I crouched down, struck the match, and held it against the balled-up newspaper. We stepped back to watch the show. The firebug, if he was awake, did not offer comment.

Katrina looped her arm around my own and leaned into me. "Where do you think Ox Haggerton went, anyway?"

"I don't know," I said. "With his personality, I'm guessing Arizona."

One of the birdhouses popped as the fire really started to take.

"I think I'll do cows next," Katrina said. "Cows made out of barbed wire. Maybe a barn, too."

I nodded. I could dig cows.

"What about you? Can I read one of your stories sometime?"

"Sure," I said. "But I'll have to write a new one first. The rest, you know … " I nodded at the fire.

"Right," Katrina said. "Well, you've got a lot of good material now, I guess."

"Maybe I'll write about a dumbshit kid who burns his own house down."

"But everybody survives, right?"

"Yeah," I said. "I guess they do."

———

It was long past dinnertime when I returned to my grand-parents' house. Grandma and Grandpa Hedley had gone to bed but my sister and father were both in the living room, watching TV and eating popcorn. They looked up when I entered the room, and I said hey. They nodded and went back to watching the movie. I'd planned on going directly out to the Grotto but I sat down on the couch instead, on the other side of Haylee with Chompy sleeping between us, lying belly-up as his forepaws twitched.

I stared at the TV but I couldn't focus on the movie. Instead I pictured our house engulfed in flames and the dark end of Haggerton's rifle. My mother lying in a hospital bed, impossibly thin and asking where I was.

Haylee reached across Chompy and held out her bowl of popcorn.

"Here," she said, keeping her gaze on the TV. "I'm full."

I took the bowl and set it on my lap. I felt an urge to bury my head in the salted popcorn and weep like a lunatic, like a real firebuggy fucker, but I took a deep breath and the feeling passed. Instead I slowly ate a few popcorn kernels, then a few more, and then I was watching the movie right along with my father and sister. Anyone passing by outside on the street might have looked in and seen a family enjoy-ing the fall evening, cozied up and lit by blue light.

Hickson's Wife

Alfred James Hickson's wife visited Balrog County ten years after his death. She was a stern, handsome woman with steely gray eyes. She arrived alone, with minimal luggage. She carried a silver single-shot pistol in her purse and spoke with a British accent that made the locals shiver and step to.

Though she'd received her husband's last letter through the post, sent on by the fellow fur trapper who'd found him tied to his death tree, Hickson's remains had already been lost to time and spotty frontier record-keeping. Mrs. Hickson had to settle for hiking around the woods in the general vicinity of his death, shooting the first raccoon she came across, and building a town upon the spot where it died.

Why Ox Saved Chompy

We can only conclude that Ox Haggerton released Chompy from his basement kennel and ran the beast off before setting our house on fire. My sister, who has brightened considerably since October, thinks our mother convinced Ox to do it. Haylee believes Mom's spirit was watching over the house and that our dog's salvation was her way of saying everything would be okay.

Yeah, well.

I don't know if I'd go that far.

What I think is that maybe old Ox once had someone truly good in his own life, somebody who'd poured enough of their love and kindness into him that it sparked forth during even his most vindictive hour. And the idea that love can be transferred, stored among the living throughout great periods of darkness and sorrow, and eventually return to the world is why, I suppose, I bothered with this accounting in the first place.

Acknowledgments

The author would like to thank his agent, Jonathan Lyons at Curtis Brown LTD, editor Brian Farrey-Latz, production editor Sandy Sullivan, publicist Mallory Hayes, book designer Steffani Pitzen, cover designer Lisa Novak (what a cool cover, right?), and everyone else at Flux. He would also like to thank Mark Rapacz, Geoff Herbach, and Dr. Mike "Miguel" Mensink, all of whom contributed in many, many outstanding ways to this fictional bug reaching the wide and crackling world.

©Todd Wardrope

About the Author

David Oppegaard is the author of *And the Hills Opened Up*, *Wormwood, Nevada*, and the Bram Stoker–nominated *The Suicide Collectors*. He lives in St. Paul, Minnesota, with his lovable cat Frenchie. David enjoys starting fires, but usually in a controlled and totally legal manner.

Visit the author online at davidoppegaard.com.